"Hi-Yo Silver!"—
the cry that brought joy
to the hearts of the oppressed,
and terror to the hearts of the evil . . .

Tonto's approach with the horses did not seem to be noticed by anyone inside the house. The Lone Ranger made quick gestures to him, signs which only Tonto could interpret. Then the masked man drew both guns, lashing at the window with one. Glass shattered into the room. The Lone Ranger's gun barked and a silver slug found its mark—the knife leaped from Lefty's hand and flashed to one side as if by magic.

Sam Slake and the other three men reached swiftly for their guns. Again flame flashed from the Lone Ranger's weapons. Then a tornado in the form of Tonto swept upon the scene, crashing through another window in a shower of glass. He did not pause when his feet struck the floor. Head down, fists knotted, he charged into the first man he saw with a force that sent the smuggler sprawling to the floor.

Tonto's fists were like battering rams driving into the faces of the men who still stood on their feet. The Lone Ranger leaped across the windowsill, shot one arm about the waist of Patricia, and lifted her bodily out of the room. He swept her onto the back of his big white stallion, while Tonto, leaping through the window and firing shots behind him, sprang onto the back of his own.

A split second before the thunder of pounding hoofs could be heard, a cry rang out in the morning air, a cry that thrilled Patricia, hearing it for the first time; a cry that filled her with courage; a cry that went a long way to offset the evil and avarice in others:

"Hi-Yo Silver! Away!"

THE LONE RANGER SERIES

THE LONE RANGER

Traps the Smugglers

Fran Striker

PINNACLE BOOKS • LOS ANGELES

THE LONE RANGER TRAPS THE SMUGGLERS

Copyright 1941 by The Lone Ranger, Inc.

A Pinnacle Books edition, published by special arrangement with Grosset & Dunlap.

First printing, September 1979

ISBN: 0-523-40491-3

Cover illustration by Bruce Minney

Printed in the United States of America

PINNACLE BOOKS, INC.
2029 Century Park East
Los Angeles, California 90067

CONTENTS

Chapter I

A SHOT IN THE NIGHT

The Lone Ranger awoke. Most men would have stirred uneasily at the shot and gone on sleeping. It was a distant shot, muffled by the steady drizzle that filled the night beyond the entrance to the cave. A habit of years awoke the Lone Ranger—an awareness of the slightest irregularity in things about him.

None of the familiar sounds of the night would break the Lone Ranger's sleep. He could slumber undisturbed through any sort of storm. The howls and cries of animals and birds would never waken him as long as those noises were a part of the natural order of things. But the bark of a gun, however faint, in the middle of the night was different.

He became wide awake without any sudden movement other than the opening of his eyes. He had an animal-like ability to waken instantly and completely with every faculty alert. His mind raced back over the memory of the shot, while his ears strained for whatever might come next.

By turning his head slightly, the Lone Ranger could look toward the depths of the cave where two horses were sheltered. The paint horse, or

1

pinto, that belonged to Tonto was quite still, but Silver, his own pure-white stallion, was tense, with ears cocked forward toward the wide mouth of the cavern.

Then the masked man noticed that Tonto's blankets had been tossed aside. The Indian was nowhere to be seen. The Lone Ranger rose to his feet and moved silently to the arching entrance. He peered into the night while rain beat upon his face.

There was no sound except the rain and the distant splashing of the Rio Grande. Yet, somewhere in the night, a shot had been fired. Someone was out there—Tonto of course—but someone else as well. What had preceded the shot? What had the Indian gone into the rain to investigate?

The Lone Ranger felt Tonto's blankets. They were still warm. Tonto's gun and gun belt were beside the blankets. The Lone Ranger pulled on his boots to start out after the unarmed Indian. He was strapping on his ivory-handled six-guns when he heard the squishing sound of someone running toward the cave on raindrenched ground. Then there was an audible gasp—a sharp intake of breath that might have been a sob. The footsteps ended with a splash.

The Lone Ranger ran toward the sound.

Overhead, according to the calendar, there was a full moon, but the banks of clouds that had rolled up at sunset had remained to blanket the sky while they dropped their cargo of rain. The light was no more than a vague, ghostly glimmer that relieved the utter blackness with a tinge of dark gray. Trees on all sides were formless blobs of black. Beyond them the wide but shallow river marked the border between two countries.

The Lone Ranger had taken perhaps a dozen steps when he saw forms that moved. An instant later he recognized the tall, broad-shouldered Indian named Tonto. Tonto seemed to be supporting a small figure.

"Who is it, Tonto?" the masked man said.

"Get to cave," replied the Indian.

Another voice, a girl's voice, broke in.

"If you'll just let me go—"

The Lone Ranger was at Tonto's side.

"Girl fall on face in mudhole," the Indian explained briefly.

"But I'm all right," the girl said, with a nervous sharpness in her voice.

"We help you," said Tonto.

"I'm not asking for help."

"We have a cave nearby," the Lone Ranger said softly. "You'll be sheltered there."

The girl began to object.

The Lone Ranger noticed that she limped as she tried to walk. "There's no place else nearby," he explained. "You can't walk far."

"I—I can try."

The small, slender girl gave a little, forced laugh.

"It—it's all so stupid of me."

"Stupid?" echoed the Lone Ranger.

"Yes, stupid is the word. I've a group of friends near here. We're camped. I—I ran away from them. Just for a lark. That's it—it was just a lark, and then I—I lost my way. I know now where I am, though. If you'll just leave me alone, I—I know I shall have no trouble getting to our camp."

The Lone Ranger on one side and Tonto on the other supported the girl as she walked toward the cave.

The masked man knew that there was little or no truth in the girl's statements. It was hardly the hour, the place, or the weather for a girl to be running away alone—for a lark.

"We'll get out of the rain," he said. "Then we can talk."

Inside the cave the girl went limp. The Lone Ranger lowered her gently to the blankets spread out on the hard-packed earth.

"We'll get some light," he said, fumbling in the darkness. He brought out a candle and some matches. In another moment a yellow gleam spread a cheery circle of light that made the cave seem almost cosy in comparison with the chilling rain and sticky mud outside.

The Lone Ranger felt the girl's pulse while Tonto looked for wounds. Aside from a slightly sprained ankle, there was apparently nothing seriously the matter.

"She's exhausted," said the Lone Ranger. "Exhausted and badly frightened. She'll regain consciousness in a moment or two."

While he bathed the girl's face with cool water the masked man asked Tonto what had transpired just before the shot that he had heard.

"Me hear man yell," said Tonto.

"Nearby?"

"Same distance as where shot fired."

"Could you understand what the man said?"

Tonto shook his head.

"Was more than one shot fired?"

"Only one."

The Lone Ranger poured more water from a canteen on the bandanna he had been using. He squeezed out the surplus moisture, then folded the

4

cloth and placed the cool pack on the unconscious girl's brow.

Though he was sure he had never seen the girl before, there was something strangely familiar about her face. The straight nose and rather pointed chin reminded him of someone he had known in the past. At the moment, he couldn't remember who it was.

Chapter II

SMUGGLER'S FRIEND

The girl sat wrapped in a blanket with her back against the wall of the cave. Sipping tea from a tin cup, she studied the masked man and Tonto with appraising eyes that were gray and steady. She had unpinned her hair to dry and it fell in a soft disorder about her shoulders, reflecting the fire in golden glints.

"I might as well be frank with you and tell you that you've done me no favor," she said.

The Lone Ranger met her gaze but made no comment.

"As a matter of fact, I'm afraid you've ruined everything."

"I'm sorry," the Lone Ranger said simply.

"What did you tell the men?"

"What men?"

"The men who came looking for me. What men do you think I'm talking about?"

The Lone Ranger shook his head.

"I don't know what men you're talking about," he said. "No one came looking for you."

The girl's eyes widened.

"Do you mean to say that Sam—er—" she faltered,

"—that a man didn't come here while I was unconscious?"

The Lone Ranger shook his head.

The girl looked toward the mouth of the cave.

"Do you think anyone has seen me here?"

"No. Tonto would have heard anyone who came near enough to see us."

"Are you sure?"

"Yes. Quite sure."

The girl's voice held a new ring.

"Tell me honestly, I must know the truth. So much depends . . ." She broke off leaving the sentence unfinished.

The Lone Ranger waited patiently, without comment.

The girl studied the leaves that remained in the bottom of her cup, as if debating whether or not to tell the man with the mask the things that were foremost in her mind. She spoke softly, almost to herself.

"There might yet be a chance to get what I came for, if it is true that no one followed me. If I could only be sure."

She placed the tin cup on the ground and looked up to meet the masked man's eyes.

"My name," she said, "is Patricia Knowlton."

"Thank you."

"I fibbed about having friends nearby."

"You didn't know who I was. I might have been an outlaw who would have been frightened away by such a fib."

The faintest trace of a smile broke the corners of the Lone Ranger's mouth.

Patricia said, "It was a rather silly notion, wasn't it? You'd hardly be frightened away by such a statement." She glanced at Tonto, then back at the Lone Ranger. "You *are* an outlaw, of course?"

"No."

"But you're masked. I always thought men who wore masks were hiding from the law."

"In one sense of the word, I'm hiding. Not because I'm an outlaw, however."

The girl was silent for a minute or two. She studied the cave, looked at the horses, then again at Tonto.

Meanwhile, the Lone Ranger tried to remember where he had heard the girl's name. There was something about "Knowlton" that struck a familiar chord, just as there had been something about the girl's face. Both the face and the name seemed to be associated with some event, long past.

"My father told me about a man who wore a mask," the girl said.

"Your father?"

A nod.

"Where is your father now?"

"He has been dead for six months."

Tonto looked up sharply.

The Lone Ranger's eyes met those of the Indian in an exchange of glances.

Patricia, not noticing the significance in the meeting of the men's eyes, continued speaking.

"Dad told me that this masked man had once been a Texas Ranger."

"Did your father tell you any more?"

"Yes. No one ever learned the name of the masked man. When he was a Texas Ranger, he was ambushed with half a dozen friends. He was the only survivor. He crept to a cave where he nearly died of wounds. An Indian friend found him there and nursed him back to health. Then this Texas Ranger concealed his identity and started out to bring the dry-gulchers to justice."

The Lone Ranger shifted his weight uneasily. He was ill at ease during the girl's narrative. He tried to change the subject.

"About that shot we heard—"

"Let me finish," said Patricia. "This masked man finally saw the last of the murderers of his friends in the hands of the law. Even then he didn't unmask. He rode away with his Indian friend. Since then he has been heard from in all parts of the West. A lot of people don't believe the stories that are told of this masked man's work. My father told me they were true stories and, in most cases, the things the masked man did were greatly underestimated."

Once more the Lone Ranger broke in.

"About your own problem—"

"My own problem can wait a while," the girl said decisively.

"This masked man became known as the Lone Ranger. It is said that he uses bullets of solid silver, but he only uses those bullets in self defense or in the defense of another man's life. Even then, he never shoots to kill. He seems to go where he can be of help. He is said to have his own particular way of serving the people of the West. He has a white horse and this Indian friend I mentioned."

The girl leaned toward the masked man. Her eyes met his squarely.

"I think," she said softly, "that *you* are the Lone Ranger."

The masked man rose to his feet. He extracted a

shiny bullet from his belt and handed it to the girl.

Patricia smiled.

"You *are* the Lone Ranger."

"I thought there was something familiar about your face. I knew your father. He was a government agent."

Patricia nodded.

"Six months ago, your father was shot in the back while trying to run down a gang of smugglers."

"That's right. They didn't have the courage to meet Dad face to face. They had to shoot him in the back without giving him a chance to defend himself."

Patricia rose to her feet and dropped the blanket from her shoulders. The smile left her face at the mention of her father. Now her eyes held a haunted, worried expression.

"I—I guess I'm sorry that you're the Lone Ranger," she said. "If you were anyone else in the world, I'd ask you to help me."

The Lone Ranger looked perplexed.

"I don't understand what you mean," he said. "Why can't you ask me to help you?"

Patricia shook her head.

"Because I—well I just can't, that's all."

She slapped at the dirt that had dried and caked on her riding clothes.

"Please don't ask for any further information. I must go."

"But where are you going?"

"Back to the cabin."

"What cabin?"

"Over there," the girl said, pointing in the general direction of the Rio Grande. "The cabin I came from."

"Look at me," the Lone Ranger said in a low, but commanding voice.

Patricia lifted her eyes. There was a hint of moisture in them.

"Thank you for what you've done."

The Lone Ranger shook his head slowly.

"I don't know about any cabin between this cave and the Rio Grande. I do know of a ranch, however. Isn't it the ranch you're going to?"

"There's no use denying that fact," Patricia said.

"That's where the shot was fired. You ran from there a little while ago."

"I can't tell you another thing," the girl said stubbornly. "I'm a double-crosser and I'm using methods that are just as unfair as any schemes Sam Slake ever—"

"Sam Slake!" broke in the Lone Ranger. "Do you mean to tell me that ranch is owned by Sam Slake?"

"I—I shouldn't have mentioned his name."

"Slake is supposed to be the leader of the pack of smugglers who killed your father—the same gang that is to blame for many murders in this part of the country."

"I'll not admit a thing," the girl cried desperately. "Let me out of this cave."

"You've gone to his ranch in the hope of getting something that will prove his guilt," the Lone Ranger said. "Isn't that the case?"

"I won't say a word."

"The shot was fired at you. When you learned that no one had followed you here, you realized that perhaps you hadn't been identified so you are going back to that ranch and have another try at whatever you're looking for."

11

"Very well," said Patricia. "You've practically guessed it all."

"Then why can't I help you?"

Tears of desperation fell from the girl's eyes.

"I have your silver bullet," she said. "I'm going to get back to Slake's house and leave the silver bullet where it can be found. They'll think you're the one who tried to steal Slake's private papers. Now do you understand? Now you see what an unprincipled creature I am. I'm going to put the blame on *you* in spite of all the kindness you've shown me."

"I think that's a very wise move."

"But don't you understand? By morning every member of Slake's gang will be hunting for you. You'll have to start now and get away from here. If you really want to help me, get away so they'll not capture you and kill you. I—I could never rest if I thought my problem had brought about the death of the Lone Ranger."

The Lone Ranger ignored the girl's plea.

"Does Sam Slake know who you are?" he asked.

"No, of course not. I'm sure he never saw me before, and he probably doesn't even know my father had a daughter."

"How did you get into the house in the first place?"

"I had to use deceit in that too. I rode past the ranch and made believe I fell from my horse. I faked an injured ankle and made Mrs. Slake take me in. None of them had a chance to see me tonight; they think I can't walk without a limp."

"How many men does Slake have with him?"

"I don't know. Several live right in the house. There are others in a bunk house."

"And what else do you know about Slake?"

12

"Only that he is utterly ruthless. He has a lot of men working for him south of the border in addition to men who work north of here, selling smuggled guns and liquor to the Indians."

The masked man nodded.

"You've learned a lot," he said.

"Enough to know that Slake is almost too powerful for the law to handle unless air-tight evidence can be found."

"Does such evidence exist?"

"It does. My father knew about it and lost his life in an attempt to get it."

The girl moved to the opening.

"I'm leaving now," she said.

The Lone Ranger made no attempt to stop her.

"Just one thing more. *Please* get away from here. Don't underestimate Slake's gang. If you're here till morning, you'll most certainly be killed."

Chapter III

A STUNNING BLOW

Two minutes after Patricia Knowlton had left the cave, the Lone Ranger was ready to follow her. He wore two heavy guns with ivory handles lashed to his thighs.

"You stay here," he told Tonto. "Watch the horses and keep the cave dark in case someone happens by."

Tonto objected. When there was a promise of action, he felt that he should be on hand.

"I know just how you feel, Tonto," the masked man said, "but this time I'll be better off traveling alone. I'm just going to make sure the girl gets back inside that house safely. I'll have a look around the place and be back here inside the hour."

As he spoke, the Lone Ranger checked his weapons and dropped them back into their respective holsters.

"I think I understand Patricia Knowlton's plan," he said. "She's going to try to complete the work her father started. She knows, just as many other people know, that Sam Slake is a smuggler, a murderer and the leader of a gang of cutthroats. She also knows that no move can be made against him legally without proof of his guilt. That's why she has managed a friendship with Slake's wife. She's living in that house, hoping to find evidence against the gang."

"Slake not know who girl is?" queried Tonto.

"If he knew that she was the daughter of a Federal operator, her life wouldn't be worth a cent. She must be using some other name while she's there."

Tonto nodded his agreement.

"Slake isn't a man to take chances. If he was suspicious about the girl, he'd kill her. What's more he'd do it so there'd be no suspicion of murder connected with him. That's why I want to be sure she gets back into her bedroom without being caught."

The masked man arranged the usual signal with Tonto. Three shots in close succession would mean that he wanted Tonto to come and bring the horses fast! Tonto nodded once again, and then the masked man stepped out of the cave.

He noted that the rain had almost stopped and the clouds were scudding across a clearing sky. The moon broke through for an instant as the Lone Ranger plunged in among the trees.

He didn't try to follow the girl's tracks. He went in a beeline toward the Rio Grande, confident that he'd sight the house when he was clear of the woods. Drops from the leafy tangle overhead splashed intermittently on the wide brim of his hat. His boots slushed thickly in the loam and mud. As he progressed he could hear the rippling of the river and judged that it must be higher than usual for the time of year.

Quite suddenly the woods ended. One moment there were dense trees on all sides, and then no trees at all. As if to aid him, the full light of the moon bathed the level land ahead and gave the Lone Ranger a clear view of the quarter-mile between him and the river's bank.

Then he saw the ranch house. It was a rambling building with a center section of two stories and a long wing on each side. The house itself was flanked by a barn and a bunk house. There were no lights to be seen in any of the windows.

The rain, before it had stopped, had washed out the footprints made by the girl in leaving the ranch. There was, however, a single set of tracks which formed a line from the woods to the house. If Sam Slake saw these in the morning, he would be instantly aware of the identity of the girl who made them. They were far too small to be mistaken for the footprints of a man.

There was no danger of prints being found in the woods. The springy, spongy carpet of leaves that had fallen through the years would not retain an indentation. The Lone Ranger affirmed this point, by touching his own footprints with his fingers. He could feel the ground returning to normal.

Something had to be done about the girl's tracks to the house.

The moon broke clear of the clouds.

The Long Ranger noted with satisfaction that the increased light made it a simple matter to see each footprint the girl had made.

He stepped from the shelter of the trees and found that his normal stride just matched the prints of the running girl. It was a simple matter to obliterate Patricia's prints by superimposing his own.

The girl's problems had become the masked man's. He wondered if Slake himself or his wife would notice the mud on Patricia's clothes and demand an explanation which couldn't be given. There were so many possible things that might trap the girl; Slake was so shrewd; it seemed impossible for Patricia to avoid discovery.

He intended to enter the house and fumble noisily until the leader of the smugglers saw him. Then when Slake had been given ample opportunity to identify the intruder as a tall man, he would escape.

The Lone Ranger reached the house and the window where the last of the footprints disappeared beneath his own. He moved slowly along the side of the building and turned the corner. Ahead of him, half way to the next corner, there was a small porch and the front door of the house.

He didn't think it necessary to look for someone crouching at the far side of the porch. There was no reason to suspect that, from this vantage point, a pair of eyes had watched him from the time he left the woods. Those same eyes watched as the masked man, crouching low, approached the porch. The owner of the eyes made no sound as he followed the Lone Ranger up the steps, a heavy gun in hand.

The top step gave a faint creak. Though it was a barely perceptible sound, the Lone Ranger heard it and whirled about. He had a flashing glimpse of a huge man with one hand raised high. He had no chance to duck or dodge the blow. The barrel of a gun crashed down on the top of his skull with a fearful impact.

The Lone Ranger crumpled. His knees bent, and he would have fallen if the assailant hadn't caught him in strong arms.

Chapter IV

BART BELDON, MANHUNTER

The Lone Ranger recovered consciousness beneath the trees in the woods. His recovery was a slow and painful procedure. His first realization was of the pain that throbbed against his temples and the base of his skull. His head ached frightfully, and for fully five minutes he lay quietly upon his back without opening his eyes. He tried desperately to gather senses that had been scattered by the force of the blow. Recollection returned slowly.

He remembered talking to a pretty girl in the cave where Tonto was, but what had happened next? How was it that he was flat upon his back? How did he get where he was? Where, in fact, was he? His brain was a jumbled confusion of innumerable questions that for some time refused to arrange themselves in any logical sequence.

Sheer will power made it possible for the Lone Ranger to concentrate his thinking faculties on one thing at a time. Caution, an instinctive caution, overruled his curiosity. He wanted to look about him, see where he was, and get his bearings. Yet he kept his eyes closed and gave no visible sign that he was conscious. He knew that he had been attacked. His frightful headache told him that. It was reasonable to suppose that his attacker was still close at hand, perhaps watching for him to return to consciousness to continue the assault. He wanted to think, or at least get his whirling senses steadied to the point where thinking might be possible, before he made a move.

He tried to remember what had happened after the scene in the cave. The girl had left, he remembered that much. Where was she going? Why had she left? The masked man had a strange sensation—a feeling that the facts, in trying to make themselves apparent, were rasping against raw nerves inside his skull. For a time pain threatened to rob him once more of his consciousness and he had to fight to keep from slipping into a black void.

There had been tracks, footprints in the mud. Now he remembered those, and recalled that he had stepped in those footprints to obliterate them. Sam Slake's house—the window through which Patricia had gone—the porch. Now it was all coming back. There had been a man at the porch. He recalled the fleeting view of an arm upraised and a flash of a gun descending with speed too great to dodge.

Where was he? That was the next question to be answered. Where was he, how had he arrived here, and who was the man who had struck him?

It was typical of the masked man to think last of all about his own condition. His first concern was the safety of Patricia Knowlton and the fear that his own predicament would increase the danger of her position.

He risked opening his eyes. He could tell by the checkered pattern of gray, moonlit sky beyond the leaves that he was in the woods. He sensed that he lay upon a blanket that had been spread out on the ground.

He turned his head to one side. Even this slight movement proved almost too much for him. New stabs of pain shot through his head and a feeling of nausea threatened for an instant to engulf him. He remained motionless until these latest torments subsided, then experimented further. Presently his head faced the clear stretch of land between the woods and Slake's house, and he determined his location.

The Lone Ranger was barely ten yards inside the edge of the woods. From here he could see between the trees that the Slake house was still in darkness. No sign of light was visible in any window. The sky was clear. The position of the moon was such that the Lone Ranger could estimate the time. It was, he reckoned, within an hour of dawn.

He thought he heard the sound of footsteps. Was this another figment of imagination, like the bells that had been ringing in his head? He closed his eyes to listen more intently. Then he was sure. Someone was approaching from within the woods.

Once more the Lone Ranger refused to obey his first impulse. Instead of turning his head in the direction of the sound to see who it was that came toward him, he kept his eyes closed and remained quite motionless and limp. He wasn't ready yet. He needed more time to regain full control of his faculties—more time to store up energy and strength against the moment when he'd have to make his break, perhaps his fight, for freedom. He took it for granted that he was a captive.

The footsteps came close to him before they

halted. He could hear the heavy breathing of a man, and then a muttered growl.

"Still out cold," a gruff voice said. "Didn't mean to hit him that hard."

It took all of the Lone Ranger's self-control to remain quiet when he felt someone's fingers on his face. For the first time he realized that he still wore his mask. Then, with a feeling of helplessness, he was aware that the fingers were unfastening it. Was his identity at last to be discovered?

But no, he rejected this possibility. Even though the moonlight was quite bright in the open, the trees shaded his hideout to such a degree that it would be impossible for anyone to see the features of his face. The mask was off! Then there came the sudden shock of cold water! The one beside the Lone Ranger was apparently concerned. The voice could be heard once more.

"Mebbe this'll bring him around."

How good that water felt! It not only eased the pain, but it seemed to shock away the last of the clouds that had been fogging the Lone Ranger's mind. The hands that applied the wet cloth were surprisingly gentle. The touch was like a woman's, in direct contrast with the man's voice and the manner in which he had wielded the clubbed gun.

The Lone Ranger's next surprising realization was that he was not tied. His hands were free to move and he moved them, with ever so much caution, a fraction of an inch at a time. Meanwhile he lifted his eyelids just enough to see through the lashes, so slowly that a casual glance would give the observer the impression that the eyes were still closed.

The man bathing his face was the same one who

21

had struck him. That much was easily seen by his size. He had those same massive shoulders and the same stiff-brimmed hat. He dipped a cloth in a cup of water and then, after wringing it, folded it and placed it across the Lone Ranger's forehead.

By this time the Lone Ranger's hand had sneaked as far as his side, and then he made another discovery. He still wore his six-guns! What manner of man was this, who knocked him out and almost killed him, and then went to such lengths to help him without taking the precaution of tying his hands or removing his guns—without, for that matter, striking a light to determine his identity? It was, of course, possible that his face had been examined by matchlight while he was unconscious, but, had this been done, it was hardly likely that the mask would have been replaced.

A bit at a time the Lone Ranger eased his left-hand gun from the holster. Only his fingers moved, while the arm gave no hint of what was taking place. After what seemed ages, he held the gun in his hand and pointed the barrel toward his captor. The big man poured more water on a cloth and was just reaching to bathe the face of the Lone Ranger when the seemingly unconscious figure reared on one elbow.

"Take it easy," snapped the Lone Ranger as he brought his gun to bear. "There's no one here but the two of us, and I have you covered."

For a moment the larger man stared in open-eyed and open-mouthed amazement. Automatically he reached for his gun. The Lone Ranger spoke again.

"Drop your gun. You're covered. If I have to, I'll shoot that gun from your hand."

The other man's gun dropped to the ground as he scrambled to his feet. The Lone Ranger, ignoring the pain in his muscles, pushed himself to a sitting posture.

"What the—" began the bulky man. "I didn't know you were conscious."

"I've been conscious long enough to appreciate the efforts you were making in my behalf," replied the Lone Ranger. "Now sit down where we can face each other. I want to talk to you."

While the other obeyed, the Lone Ranger found his mask where it had been dropped beside him on the blanket and adjusted it across his eyes.

"First of all," the heavily built man said, "I want you to understand that I'm not in the habit of dropping my gun when I'm told to. I did it in this case, because I know blamed well that you'd not only try to shoot it out of my hand, you'd do it, and that'd wreck the shootin' iron. I don't hanker to have it wrecked because I'm goin' to be needin' it aplenty before very long."

"How did you know I'd succeed if I aimed at it?"

"Because I had the chance to find out who you are."

A frown crossed the face of the masked man. "You," he said softly, "know who I am?"

"I mean to say, I know you're the gent that's called the Lone Ranger."

"How do you know that?"

"At first, when I cracked you with my gun, I thought you were a crook—a particular crook that I'm downright anxious to get hold of. I wanted to get you alone and get you tellin' me a lot of things I want to know. I dragged you away from the house over yonder, hoisted you to the back of my horse,

23

and then brought you here to the woods. I found out you weren't the one I thought you were, in short order."

"How did you find that out?" demanded the Lone Ranger, still holding his gun steady.

"Easy. The crook I want has an unmistakable scar that starts at one side of his nose and goes all the way down to his jaw—an old knife wound that didn't heal good. When I found out you weren't that hombre, the next thought was, 'who are yuh?'"

The speaker paused.

"Go on," the Lone Ranger said.

"I struck matches an' examined your guns because sometimes a man has his hame or his initials on his six-guns. You didn't have anythin' like that, but you sure did have as pretty a brace of shootin' irons as I've ever come across. When I looked at the bullets I noted there was somethin' odd about them. They didn't look like any lead I'd ever seen. Then it struck me that they were made of silver! Then I guessed who you were."

"So you took off my mask?"

"No!" said the other emphatically. "I did nothin' of the sort. I sure wanted to! I realized the chance I had to see what no one else, as far as I know, has ever seen. All I had to do to get a look at your face was to take that mask off, then strike matches an' study you. But I didn't do it. Instead I examined your skull to see if it was cracked where I hit you an' found that it seemed to be all right. I guess your hat must have saved you. Then I spread a blanket an' stretched you on it, an' went for some water. I had to take the mask off to bathe your face, but I didn't make no light to look at you. That's the whole of the story an' you can take my

24

word for it. In case you're interested, my name is Bart Beldon, an' any man will tell you that there ain't a more honest man alive than Bart Beldon."

"Bart Beldon," said the Lone Ranger, repeating the name. "I've heard of you."

"You have?"

The Lone Ranger nodded, then realized that it was too dark for Beldon to see the gesture.

"Yes," he said.

"Where?"

"Your work has made you fairly well known, Beldon. You're a government official. You're working against a gang of smugglers."

"That's right."

"You're said to be a dangerous man in any kind of a fight, but one of the squarest men alive. I'm sorry I had to use a trick to get the drop on you, but I guess you can understand why I did it."

"Sure I can," said Beldon heartily.

The Lone Ranger holstered his gun and stuck his hand out toward the other. "I'm glad to meet you," he said.

"Well, I'm downright proud to meet you," said Beldon, gripping the masked man's hand. "Proud! That's the word. I'm sorry I cracked you on the head."

"Who did you think I was?"

"A critter by the name of Ponsonby. Ever happen to hear of him?"

"What's his other name?"

"Luther—Luther Ponsonby."

"Never heard of him. Is he one of Sam Slake's men?"

"I can't tell you any more about him right now," said Beldon, "except this. He's built about the same

25

as you. That's why I made the mistake of capturin' you."

Bart Beldon rose to his feet, came close to the Lone Ranger, then squatted on his haunches. His face was within two paces. He gripped his pistol, and the ugly snout of it was less than six inches from the Lone Ranger's eyes.

"I'm sorry," Beldon said grimly, "I don't like to do what I'm goin' to, but it's got to be done."

"What's this for, Beldon?"

"I'm takin' your guns, Lone Ranger, an' puttin' handcuffs on you."

"Have you gone crazy?"

"Nope." Beldon slipped the masked man's guns from their leather holsters with deft movements and tossed them to one side. Then he stepped back and from somewhere about his person he produced a pair of handcuffs.

"I thought you were a square shooter, Beldon. This is hardly square, after I lowered my gun because I trusted you."

"I didn't make any promises," said Beldon. He locked the handcuffs in place with quick clicks, then dropped his gun in the holster and produced a rope.

"I've got to rope you to the tree behind you for the time bein', partner, an' I'm honest when I say I hate to do it. I wouldn't do it, if it wasn't for Miss Patricia."

"What about her?"

"She's over yonder in the Slake house, an' the girl's in danger."

"I know that!"

"I figgered you did. That's why you was there, ain't it?"

26

"Yes."

"I saw her come out of the woods a while ago, then I saw you followin' her. I figured you were up to no good."

The Lone Ranger nodded.

"The girl has to be gotten out of that house. I've got my plans all made to go there an' call on Slake an' see about gettin' the girl before Slake finds out who she is. I don't want you tryin' to help me an' doin' nothin' but hinderin' me."

As he spoke, Beldon's hands were busy. He performed a quick and effective job of roping, and then stood up.

"Hold on," the Lone Ranger said. "How do you plan to help Patricia Knowlton?"

"I'm goin' there as soon as it gets day when the folks are up an' about."

"Then what?"

"I'll let on that I don't know who Sam Slake is, but that I'm huntin' a girl by the name of Maud an' have a warrant to arrest her. I'll claim that Miss Patricia is named Maud Miller an' put her under arrest. That'll get her out of the house. Then I can go there with a group of men, crack down on Sam Slake, an' search the house for evidence against him."

"Confound it, Beldon, don't you realize what such a move will mean?"

"What's your notion?"

"Slake is no fool! He's well advised, and he'll know exactly who you are as soon as you go to that house!"

"He won't know me."

"But he will," insisted the Lone Ranger, "and he'll see through the scheme at once! He'll know

27

then that Patricia is the daughter of your old partner, Knowlton! And both you and the girl will die!"

"I'll take the chance that my way is the right way," Bart Beldon said doggedly. "We're goin' to close in on the Slake house an' that girl's got to be out of there before the shootin' starts. I know better than to try just askin' her to leave, so I'll put her under arrest an' take her. She never should have tried to carry on her father's work."

While he waited for dawn and signs of activity that would show the Slake household to be up and about the chores, Bart Beldon told how he had men camped and waiting not far from the Slake ranch. He explained how his plan was calculated to work. Once the girl was out of the house, the men would close in, arrest everyone in sight and search the place from roof to foundation for evidence against Slake and the smugglers.

"But," interposed the Lone Ranger at one point, "what will you do if you don't find the evidence you want?"

"We'll find it. Slake has to keep some sort of account books or records. He's got to have some names and locations, and he couldn't run his business without a lot of other details."

"I asked what you'd do if you didn't find that evidence. Do you think he'd keep it in that house of his?"

"Where else?"

A light in one window of the cabin brought an abrupt end to the discussion. Beldon ducked back among the trees and came out with his horse. As he mounted he said:

"I'll turn you loose when I come back."

The Lone Ranger watched the receding figure of

28

the government man in the gray light of dawn. He tried the handcuffs and found them tight. He strained against the rope that held him. This too was firm and gave no hope of freedom. Exerting more strength, the masked man tugged and pulled against the loops of steel. He fought and strained until the skin was broken, without the slightest measure of success. His efforts brought gasps from lips that were pinched. One thought remained foremost in his mind.

"Patricia Knowlton will be killed."

Chapter V

SLAKE SHOWS HIS HAND

Bart Beldon's fist thundered with official force on the heavy door of the kitchen. A woman's voice inside called:

"Who's there?"

"It's the law," replied the big man. "I'm here with a warrant for the arrest of Maud Miller. Open up!"

A rustle of steps sounded from the house. Then the woman called again:

"What's that name?"

"Maud Miller."

"Ain't no one here by that name."

"I don't know what name she's usin' now, but open the door an' I'll describe her." Beldon shifted his weight from one foot to the other, and with great deliberation filled and lighted his pipe.

There was a lengthy pause. He saw a shadow on the window to his left and knew that someone was there, looking out, to study him and determine whether or not he came alone. He stepped back to give the one inside a better view of him without betraying the fact that he knew he was being watched. Then new steps came to the door and a moment later it swung open. Sam Slake himself stood just inside.

"Well, come in," said Slake in a high-pitched, nasal voice. "Come in if yer goin' to."

Beldon advanced a step, closed the door with his heel and stood with his back against it. His left hand held the blackened bowl of his pipe, his right was hooked by a thumb to his belt, just an inch from the butt of his gun.

"Yore name's Bart Beldon, ain't it?"

"That's right. An' you, I guess, are Sam Slake."

Slake nodded a head that was bald except for a fringe of jet black hair above each ear. Beldon would have been disappointed in finding so lean and emaciated an individual if he had not known from descriptions what to expect. Slake was less than average height, and lean for his size at that. His face had the pinched look of a man who has been half starved, and his eyes had a dull glazed look. He certainly did not look like the leader of one of the best organized, most ruthless, and most daring gangs in the southwest. It was hard to believe that his genius for organization had built a gang of smugglers that extended from the purchasers of goods, as far south as Mexico City, to the salesmen in Kansas.

"What's this you said about Maud Miller?"

As Beldon drew an official-looking document from the inside pocket of his coat, and handed it to Slake, the door to a room on his left creaked softly. Beldon knew that one of Slake's guards was hidden there, holding a six-gun or rifle in readiness. He knew that he would be covered every minute of the time and that the slightest careless move might start guns roaring.

He assumed an air of complete indifference. Gazing idly at the ceiling, he exhaled a cloud of smoke, while Slake examined the document.

"This here is a warrant fer the arrest of a woman named Maud Miller," said Sam Slake.

"That's right," agreed Bart Beldon.

"What's this paper got to do with me? I dunno anyone with a name like that."

"No more do I," broke in Slake's slatternly wife, who stood by the stove in the background.

"I guess this here woman changes her name as often as she does her clothes," said Beldon amiably. "I've sure had a hard time trackin' her down. I expect she's schemin' to do you folks in, the same as she has a lot of other people in this part of the country."

"Do *me* in?" Slake's comment invited Beldon to tell more about the girl.

"Yes indeed," said Beldon. "She has a way of gettin' friendly with people that own a prosperous lookin' piece of land, then movin' in with 'em till she finds out where they hide their savin's."

"Steals from 'em?" asked Slake.

"That's what the charge is. I aim to take her back to Eagle Pass when I find her."

"What makes you think she's here with us?"

"All I know is that a report come to our office that a girl of her description was livin' here with you. Now you saw the description on that paper, Slake. If it fits the girl that's here, then let me talk to her. If it don't, or if you know that your wife's friend ain't the one we want, then I'll shove on. How did you come to know the girl?" The last query was addressed to Mrs. Slake.

"She had a fall from her horse a couple of weeks

32

ago. There wasn't nothin' to do but fetch her in here."

Beldon nodded.

"That's how this Maud Miller works all right enough."

Mrs. Slake glanced at her husband.

"Might be he's right at that."

"I'll handle this—you handle the breakfast!" snapped Sam Slake in an unpleasant voice. He turned to Beldon. "Tell me—how is it that a Federal agent is concerned with house robbin'?"

"This is sort of a special case."

"I thought the only thing you men cared about was things such as smugglin', an' sellin' likker tuh redskins, an' things o' that sort."

Bart Beldon repeated himself.

"It's a sort o' special case." His voice became official. "I'm not in a position to divulge the information we have, but you see, Slake, I—well I guess you're smart enough so all I have to do is give you a hint. Uncle Sam is interested in puttin' counterfeiters in jail."

"So this Maud Miller is wanted for counterfeitin'?"

"I ain't said so."

"Is she or ain't she?"

"I ain't at liberty to say no more. Now will you let me have a talk with her?"

"Step into the next room," invited Sam Slake. "Ahead of me."

Bart Beldon detected a peculiar quality in Sam Slake's voice. Slake walked behind him as he pushed boldly through the door from the kitchen into the room beyond.

Dawn, slanting through the windows, gave the

place a dismal light. There was one huge table in the center of the room, around which were ranged at least a dozen chairs. Slake motioned to one of them.

"Sit down."

Bart Beldon sat. Slake started across the room, paused, and turned back.

"By the way," he said, "did you ever know a gent by the name o' Knowlton?"

The question, though seemingly casual, struck Beldon forcibly. He tried to answer in an equally casual vein. "I've heard of him. We never worked together though."

"Never?" Slake's eyes bored directly into Beldon's.

Beldon shook his head with an indifferent manner that gave no trace of the tension he felt. How much did Slake know and how much did he suspect? Was his query about Knowlton as casual as he had made it sound?

Once more Beldon heard the barely perceptible creaking of a door followed by a squeak from a loose floor board. He sensed that someone had entered the room. He felt, even though he heard no further sound, that one or more men were creeping close behind him. When he became sure of this fact, it was too late.

Strong arms gripped him from in back and pinioned his elbows to his sides. A rope was tossed about him before he could even begin to struggle, and at the same instant he felt a hard cloth jerked about his face to cover his mouth as a sort of partial gag. Sam Slake leaned forward, talon-like hands clutching at Bart Beldon's throat. "You try an' fight," he snarled, "an' we'll choke you here an' now."

Beldon could not have made a statement or asked a question if he had wanted to. The gag took care of that. He could only listen to what Sam Slake said.

"If what you told us is the truth, there ain't nothin' to be worried about, but I aim to find out if it is the truth. There was a few things about that girl that spilled from her hoss that didn't strike me as on the level. The story she told sounded sort o' made up. Now mebbe the reason fer that is what you say, but, on t'other hand, mebbe what you said ain't the case. Mebbe it's somethin' different."

Slake straightened and waited for the three men who had entered the room to complete their job of roping. Then he said:

"Some time durin' the night, I heard sounds in my office an' went to see what was makin' 'em. The squeakin' door gave me away an' the prowler, whoever it was, got out the window. I found that my desk was bein' looked over. Well, I hanker to know more about things."

Beldon's eyes met those of Sam Slake. Slake went on speaking.

"I made mention of a gent named Knowlton. Now it comes to me that Knowlton had a girl—a daughter. She was jest about the same age as the girl that's here. Mebbe that'll give you somethin' nice to think about while I go an' have a little talk with her."

Slake reached out and helped himself to Beldon's own six-gun. He "broke" the weapon, examined the load, then closed and cocked it. A moment later the gun spoke with a roar. Sam Slake laughed and walked from the room, still holding Bart Beldon's smoking weapon.

Chapter VI

TRAPPED

Patricia Knowlton held her riding clothes out the window, brushing vigorously to remove the last traces of mud from her adventure in the night. She heard the bark of the gun, muffled by the heavy walls of the solidly built house, but attached little importance to it. Gunfire was frequent about the Slake house. There were many rattlers and small animals about and it was customary for the men to take pot shots at them.

There was, however, something ominous about the rap on her door a few seconds after the gun's report. Pat closed the window softly.

"What is it?" she asked.

"I want to speak to you, Miss," said Slake's voice.

"Just a minute." Patricia glanced at the mirror on her way to the door. She met Sam Slake with a smile that she hoped looked genuine. "Is breakfast ready?"

"They's a little matter I want to speak about before breakfast, Miss."

"I hope there's nothing wrong."

"Mebbe so, mebbe not. Did you hear anythin' durin' the night?"

"Nothing that sounded unusual. Why?"

"No gunshot?"

"I did hear a gun, but your wife told me that the men often fired their guns. In fact there was another shot just a moment ago."

"The men don't shoot in the middle o' the night, unless they's a mighty good reason. It was me that fired durin' the night. Know why?"

"How would I know?"

"I'll tell you why, Miss. It was because they was someone tryin' to bust intuh my desk an' git at my private papers."

"A thief?" Patricia exclaimed, trying to show alarm. "I hope nothing was stolen."

"Nothin' was stole, but the critter got away from me. Now, seein' that they ain't no cash to speak of in the house, I wonder why a thief would come here?"

Patricia forced a laugh. "I'm a poor one to answer that," she said.

"Yuh sure you can't answer it?"

"Mr. Slake, just what are you driving at? You act as if you suspected me of—of something."

"I jest hope that prowler ain't no friend of yours, Miss. If he was, then you're due fer some mighty unpleasant news. We got him."

"Y-you what?"

"You heard the shot jest now."

Patricia felt as if the walls of the house were closing in upon her. Sam Slake could mean no one but the Lone Ranger. Her throat constricted. Her lips, she knew, were trembling. The Lone Ranger, most heroic figure in all the West, dead because of her! It wasn't possible. It couldn't be. Why had he come to the house?

Slake misunderstood the girl's emotion. He grinned in a way that made Patricia shudder. His teeth were brownish yellow with tobacco stain and pointed like a wolf's fangs. He saw the startled expression on the face of the girl, and said:

"Yuh don't need tuh answer. The look on yer face is answer aplenty."

Patricia tried with small success to compose herself.

"What do you want me to say?" she asked.

"I guess there ain't nothin' you need to say. I was aimin' to ask you what the hombre wanted here, but now it seems that he come here to help you. Well, that'll do fer Mister Bart Beldon."

The name meant nothing to Patricia.

"Who?" she demanded.

"Bart Beldon. Why?"

"You mean—is it—" The girl floundered for words. Her mind had been conjuring up visions of the Lone Ranger sprawled dead on the floor of the next room.

"Bart Beldon is the man you've shot?" she finished finally.

"Sure it is." Slake frowned upon the girl, his smile gone now. "Who'd you think I was talkin' about?"

"I—I guess I didn't know."

"I was talkin' about the Federal man, Bart Beldon, an' you knew it. You knew he come here to get you out o' the way, an' when yuh heard that shot an' found that it was Beldon that'd been drilled, an' not one of my men, you was mighty startled lookin'. That was where you tipped yer hand. You showed me that you an' Beldon was workin' tuhgether. If

39

it'd been otherwise, you wouldn't o' been concerned about his bein' hurt."

The girl tried to adjust her composure. She realized that she had been tried by a most peculiar set of circumstances. Her concern for the Lone Ranger had showed in her face, and the expression had been interpreted by Slake as applicable to Bart Beldon. This had made Slake suspect an alliance between Beldon and the girl, and, indeed, she could not deny that she knew him. If she tried to explain that she had misunderstood the identity of the victim of the gunfire, it would serve no good purpose, but would only implicate the Lone Ranger as well as Beldon. The damage had been done and Slake had what he considered sufficient verification of his suspicions.

The grin reappeared on Slake's face as he drew his gun and steadied it on the girl.

"Don't get too worried," he told her. "Beldon ain't dead yet. I jest told you about that shot to see how you'd act an' you acted jest like I figgered yuh would. Walk straight ahead o' me."

Slowly, in something of a daze, the girl obeyed. Slake followed close behind her, the muzzle of his gun against the small of her back.

"Now that we know how things stand," he said, "we'll have the showdown, an' I reckon there'll be some accidents around this part of the country."

Patricia walked across the living room, recalling what her father had told her about the "accidents" that happened around the Sam Slake domain— "accidents" that involved falling into ravines, drowning, drinking poisoned water, and countless other forms of what, for lack of proof of anything else, had to be called "accidents."

40

She halted at the door.

"Go on," said Slake. "The Beldon gent is right there in the next room. Step through an' have a look at him."

Chapter VII

SLAKE MAKES A PROPOSITION

Beldon's eyes met those of Patricia Knowlton without any change in expression. The girl glanced first at him, and then at the three men who were in the dining room with him. The trio had, in common, a cruel and unkempt aspect. Faces that were unshaved and unwashed framed red-rimmed and bloodshot eyes. They were fully dressed, and each man wore two guns.

"Take the gag off him," ordered Sam Slake.

The tallest and leanest of the men drew a long, slim-bladed knife from a leather contrivance that he wore beneath the sleeve of his flannel shirt. He made a quick pass at the back of Bart Beldon's head, and the cloth that had gagged the man dropped to his lap. The knife expert grinned in pride at his deftness.

"Never touched flesh," he commented returning the blade to its scabbard.

Patricia fancied that the man could have sliced a gash across a man's throat with the same unconcern. Slake explained:

"Lefty is one o' the best knife men I ever seen. I'd sooner face another man with a brace o' six-guns than face Lefty with that toad stabber o' his."

Slake turned to Beldon. "Now that you're free to talk, Beldon, you might tell me why you come here."

"None of yer business," snarled Bart Beldon in a tone that was just as uncompromising as that used by Slake.

Slake thought for a moment. To Patricia he said:

"Sit down, Miss, this here is likely to be quite a sizable talk before we get done." The girl took a place on one of the chairs while Slake drew another chair close enough to him to place one foot upon the seat. He rested his elbow on the knee that was bent.

"None of my business eh, Beldon? Now, that ain't the way it strikes me. Seems to me like it's plenty of my business when you come here with a faked warrant an' a pack o' lies." He looked at his three hired killers. "Don't it strike you boys that it's my business?"

There were nods from the men. Lefty, the knife wielder, grinned at the mood of his boss. Slake was in one of his bantering frames of mind, in which he enjoyed toying with the emotions of his helpless victims much as a cat will toy with a wounded mouse before striking the final blow. Lefty anticipated amusement.

"Anyhow," continued Slake, "I'm goin' to make it my business. Now then, Beldon, either you're mighty stupid an' dumb, or you think I am. You figgered that you could come here an' make a play to git the girl out of this house without me suspectin' anythin'. Well that was yer first mistake. I make it my business to know who's workin' fer the government an' what they look like. I knew you the minute I seen you—an' I knew what you come here for. If you'd flashed a search warrant an' said you'd come to go through this house an' hunt fer evidence that'd tie me into some smugglin' activities, I'd o' knowed you was speakin' the truth. But it didn't ring true when you come here an' made out you didn't even suspect me of anythin' out o' line. That was yer second mistake, an' it was all that was needed to get me thinkin'.

"When I started thinkin', I asked myself why you'd want to get the girl out of this house. Well, the answer to that was easy. She was in the way of what you figgered on doin'. You must've figgered on comin' here to try an' arrest me, an' looked for some gunplay. You didn't want the Knowlton girl to git hurt, so you schemed to get her out in the only way that you could. Ain't that right?"

"You know blamed well it's right," retorted Beldon.

Slake grinned. "It was a slick scheme, Beldon, a mighty slick scheme. The girl couldn't give no argument at all. If she tried to say she wasn't Maud Miller, it'd be right in line with what you tried to make me believe. The only trouble was that I saw through the scheme. Now, havin' seen through it that far, I c'n see that you were readyin' to try an' arrest me. Now you ain't such a fool that you'd try an' arrest me without havin' evidence ag'in me."

Beldon had no evidence against Sam Slake but he had determined to make a bold play in the hope that fortune would favor him and put him in possession of evidence when he had made the arrest. He had reason to suppose a raid upon the ranch would produce such evidence. Luther Ponsonby was the key man. Luther Ponsonby! Where was he?

44

Beldon had supposed that Ponsonby would be among the men in the house or on the premises, but he hadn't yet seen anyone who wore the scar that would identify the one he sought.

Slake continued speaking. It wasn't until he mentioned Luther Ponsonby that Beldon paid particular attention to his words.

"Ponsonby," Slake was saying, "is a double-crossin' rat. I found out that he was willin' to sell me out an' turn over some evidence against me. Now it's plain as day that you've located Ponsonby, an' that you've got that evidence."

"What makes you so sure of that?" inquired Beldon.

"You wouldn't figger to arrest me without havin' the evidence."

"Perhaps I thought I'd find Luther Ponsonby here."

Slake shook his head.

"Don't try to make me think that. You know as well as I do that Ponsonby ain't here and hasn't been here for two weeks. You got him hid somewhere so's I can't get at him."

Beldon's face did not betray his thoughts. Slake had admitted that there was evidence against him— admitted that Luther Ponsonby had that evidence. This was an admission of importance, if only Beldon could make use of it. He glanced at the window, then at the men in the room, and measured his chances of escape.

His hands were tied, but he was free to use his legs. If he could leap through the window and, by a miracle, escape the forthcoming fusillade of gun-fire, he might make the woods. It was a slim, a very slim, an almost hopeless chance, but it was the only one he had. Even this, however, would leave Patricia in peril.

"Now then, Beldon," said Slake, "I'm goin' to make a proposition to you."

Beldon's eyes moved from the window to the speaker.

"Proposition?"

Slake nodded. He glanced at Patricia.

"Nice girl."

"What about that proposition, Slake?"

As if he hadn't heard, Slake continued.

"It'd be a shame for her to die so young, wouldn't it, though?"

"How about that proposition?" repeated Beldon.

"Oh, yes, I'm gettin' to that. You went to a lot o' trouble to protect the girl's life. Her life means somethin' to you, don't it?"

"Well?"

"I've got somethin' you want, Beldon, in a way o' speakin'. I've got the life o' this girl. You got somethin' I want. You got the evidence that'd put me in jail."

"I savvy. You figure you'll spare the life of the girl, if I turn over the evidence against you, isn't that it?"

"That," said Slake, "is it."

"How do I know you'll keep your word?" asked Beldon.

"You don't. You do know that the girl ain't got a chance unless I do git that evidence. You ain't got a chance, either. The two of you are here in this house, an' there ain't a chance of either of you gittin' out alive unless I say so."

"You'd let me go to get the evidence?"

Slake shook his head. "Couldn't take the risk.

You'd have to write a note to whoever has got it an' let one o' my men take the note. When he got back I'd turn the girl loose."

"*No!*" cried Patricia. "I won't hear of such a thing. If you have any evidence that will jail this pack of cutthroats, in the name of mercy let that evidence be used! If you and I die here, there will be others to carry on."

All eyes were turned on the girl as she spoke. Her face was flushed with excitement and her eyes were fearless.

Patricia stood facing Bart Beldon.

"You listen to me," she cried. "I came here to get evidence against this gang. My father knew there was such evidence and he tried to get it himself. He was murdered. I came here and I knew the risk I ran. I was willing to run that risk. I don't care what happens to me; I'm interested only in seeing Sam Slake and all the rest of his gang get what's coming to them. I want this gang to hang! I won't trade my life for theirs!"

For a fleeting moment there was admiration in the face of Sam Slake as he looked at the girl. Then his expression changed to a dark scowl.

"Lefty," he said.

"Yeah, boss."

"Bring out that knife."

The blade flashed in the slanting rays of the rising sun.

"Lay it against the girl's throat."

Lefty appeared to enjoy the act. The cold steel made Patricia wince inwardly, but she didn't exhibit the slightest sign of fear. Instead her lips drew back and her white teeth flashed in a laugh that was devoid of humor.

47

"Go on," she cried. "Go on, you pack of snakes! Kill me and see what it gets you! I'm satisfied to know that the law at last has what it needs to rid Texas of your wolf-pack!"

Beldon himself knew otherwise. He would have given his eyesight to bring about the condition that Patricia thought existed. There was no evidence against Sam Slake. There would be none until the man called Luther Ponsonby was found. Even if he had desired to do so, Beldon could not barter for the girl's life.

"Make up your mind," said Slake.

Beldon stared as if he couldn't believe the cruelty he saw.

"His mind," said Patricia, "is already made up. Do you think you can bargain with men who have given their word to uphold the law—men whose word means something? Beldon would sooner die a thousand deaths and have me do the same, than buy our lives in the way you suggest."

"There ain't a man alive that c'n sit there an' see what Beldon'll see without breakin'," replied Slake. "I know he wouldn't deal with us to save his own life, but it ain't only his life that's in danger." He swung toward Beldon. "I'm givin' Lefty the word to start workin' in jest five seconds, Beldon. Make up yer mind fast."

Beldon's brain raced frantically in search of some way to postpone the fate that was so close at hand.

"Wait!" he fairly shouted.

Sam Slake grinned confidently.

"What sort of note d'you want me to write, Slake?"

"You know what to write an' who to write it to. You know where that evidence is at."

48

"Beldon," cried Patricia, "don't you do it. Remember your oath!"

"Oath be hanged. I'm not sittin' here an' seein' you killed. Slake, I can't write with my hands tied."

"Untie his hands," Slake ordered the chunky man beside the law officer. "But draw yer gun an' keep it leveled on him."

"Bart Beldon," Patricia shouted, "if you try to save me by any such means, I promise you it'll do no good."

"But—" began Bart Beldon.

"I swear to you I've never in my life made a promise I haven't kept. I've never given my word lightly and I've never said what I haven't meant. Now listen to me before you write and sign any paper. If you buy my freedom in this way, I won't *want* to live! My father *died* trying to put these men in jail. Don't you understand that? He *died* to get the evidence you have. Are you going to give up what my father died trying to get?"

Beldon's face was beaded with sweat. His muscles twitched under the strain. He found that his hands were free, and gathered himself for a leap at Sam Slake. If only he could snatch a gun, get the muzzle against Slake's head and be ready to shoot if any further move was made against the girl.

Slake seemed to read Bart Beldon's mind.

"Keep that blade right where it is," he said to Lefty. "At the first quick move on Beldon's part, let her have it."

"I will," promised Lefty.

"You," said Slake to Beldon, "start writin'."

A pad of paper and a pencil were held out to the official.

"Coward!" taunted Patricia. "You *can't* be that

49

much of a coward, Bart Beldon. *Please* don't turn my respect for your badge into contempt."

Hardly aware of what he did, Bart Beldon took the pad and pencil. He glanced at the scornful eyes of the girl. Looking at Slake he saw a grin of confidence.

"Go on an' write," Slake said.

Lefty's knife hand was steady.

The steel edge touched Patricia's throat.

Beldon's glance shifted toward the window of the room. He dropped his eyes quickly, lest they betray what he had seen. His lips compressed and his fingers took a firmer grip on the pencil. He put the point to paper, but he did not write. Instead, he waited, scarcely breathing. He had seen what he least expected to see—the head and shoulders of a man who wore a mask across his eyes.

Chapter VIII

HI-YO SILVER, AWAY!

After the Lone Ranger had brought blood to his wrists in his efforts to rid himself of the handcuffs and had given up the task as hopeless, he concentrated on the rope that bound him to the tree.

His head still ached frightfully from the blow Bart Beldon had administered. Each time he strained against the ropes the throbbing in his temples was increased tenfold. There were times when he had to close his eyes and rest his head against the trunk of the tree to stave off a giddiness that might have meant unconsciousness and a loss of valuable time.

The masked man knew that Tonto would come in search of him if he did not return to the cave by daybreak, but he had no intention of waiting if he could free himself first. He thought of shouting for the help he sorely needed, but that would only serve to notify Bart Beldon and perhaps the Sam Slake gang that he had an ally. A cry for aid was likely to defeat his own purpose by ultimately bringing about the capture of Tonto.

The handcuffs that connected the Lone Ranger's wrists permitted his hands to rest in his lap. The rope that held him to the tree was passed six times across his chest and upper arms. His biceps were held tightly to his ribs, while his back was pressed against the base of the big elm. Beldon had made him as comfortable as security would permit. He sat on Beldon's blanket and could have been quite at ease, might easily have slept without discomfort, if he had not wanted so desperately to get loose.

He gathered his strength and strained once more against the ropes. His head was pressed back against the tree and his chest thrown hard against the lashing. He strained with his arms, forcing every ounce of strength against the ropes. His face grew red, then purple, with exertion. He drew great gulps of air into his lungs, then held his breath to add power to his straining.

There wasn't a chance of breaking that rope. There was a chance, however, that it might be stretched. He did not need to stretch it much. A tiny bit would do for the plan he had in mind.

He relaxed and found that the rope was just a shade less tight than it had been before. He let the last bit of air out of his lungs, collapsing his broad chest as much as possible, and then made his arms go limp. He slid down, hunching his hips forward and away from the tree. By wriggling his arms and shoulders, he found that the rope could be slid upwards a fraction of an inch at a time. Encouraged, the masked man continued his maneuvers, disregarding the painful complaint of tortured muscles, the splitting headache, and the stinging agony in his badly chafed wrists. The rope slipped over one shoulder, and he could bring his arms into use. It was but the matter of a moment, now that he could use his hands, to lift the coils over his head. Still handcuffed, his wrists bound together, the Lone Ranger was free to stand, to gether up his guns and hat, and beat his way through the woods to the cave.

The happiness on Tonto's face at the return of the masked man gave way to concern at the condition his friend was in.

"Never mind about me," said the Lone Ranger, in reply to the Indian's worried question. "There's nothing the matter that time won't take care of. I've got to get these handcuffs off."

Tonto threw some dry wood on the glowing coals and gave close attention to the manacles.

"Take plenty long," he said. "Me got file, but take long time."

"Never mind getting them off my wrists, just break the chain so I can use my hands separately. I'll wear the things as a bracelet on each arm until we catch up with Bart Beldon."

At the mention of the name the Indian's eyes looked up inquiringly.

"A government official, Tonto, and one who is likely to bring about the murder of the girl who was here last night. Where is your axe?"

Tonto scurried toward the side of the cave where the duffle of the two was stored. He brought forth a keen-edged axe, the short handle of which made the packing of the tool a simple matter. Meanwhile the Lone Ranger had selected a rock with a flat top. He placed his hands on this and drew them as far apart as the links between the cuffs would permit.

"Now," he said, "swing hard. No light blow will cut through that steel!"

Tonto frowned. He studied the length of chain.

There was scarcely an inch between the masked man's hands. To swing hard enough to break the chain meant a full overarm blow with the axe. The blow, if misdirected by half an inch, would slice the Lone Ranger's hand from wrist to fingers.

"Go on, Tonto," the masked man said.

Tonto shook his head slowly. "Not like," he muttered.

"You never miss your mark. Come, break that chain before Patricia Knowlton dies."

Tonto's mouth was firmly clamped. His strong hands gripped the axe and swung it overhead. The light of the campfire glanced off the edge of the blade as it flashed down. Sparks flew from steel and the flint rock beneath it. There was a metallic ring like that of a hammer on a blacksmith's anvil. The Lone Ranger's hands jerked apart and Tonto grinned.

"Me glad that done," the red man said.

But Tonto wasn't idle. He dropped the axe and in less time than it takes to tell he gripped the wrists of his strong white friend and looked at them. He brought cloths and water and bathed the places where the skin was torn, then slid the handcuffs higher on the wrists and put bandages in place.

"I'll not be any too fast on the draw while those bandages are there, Tonto," the Lone Ranger said. "If there's any occasion for fast gunplay, I—"

Tonto interrupted. "Tonto do."

A slight smile crossed the Lone Ranger's face. Then he and Tonto worked as a team. They hurriedly packed up to get ready for travel.

"We'll not come back here," the Lone Ranger said.

"Where go?"

"First of all, we're going to send Patricia Knowlton away. That girl has too much courage for her own good. She can't be allowed to mix into the Sam Slake gang."

Tonto agreed.

"Then we're going to see about Bart Beldon. I don't know how much evidence he has against Slake, but I'd be willing to bet it isn't enough to get a conviction in a court of law. Slake is too clever to let *anyone* get that much evidence against him."

"What do about Sam Slake?"

"Slake's gone too far, Tonto; he's got to be captured. Not just Slake, either. I want to see a roundup of all the smugglers, liquor-sellers, gun-peddlers, and killers who work with him and for him."

"How we get evidence?"

"I don't know yet," replied the Long Ranger shaking his head slowly, "but we're going to find a way."

As they talked they packed the horses with easy skill. Silver, the fastest horse in the entire West, looked rested and fit. Scout, the paint that Tonto rode, was only a shade smaller than the big white stallion, and he, too, looked eager to be out of the cave and in motion.

Instead of mounting, the Lone Ranger gathered up the reins and led Silver from the cave. Tonto followed close behind, pausing just long enough to empty the canteen on what was left of the fire.

It had taken longer to get the horses packed than the Lone Ranger realized. There were streaks of light in the sky when he and Tonto left the woods and started across the level, open stretch of land

55

toward the ranch house. There were lights, not only in the kitchen, but also in several other windows of the house.

The Lone Ranger went on foot, leaving Tonto instructions to bring both horses and follow at a distance so that the hoofbeats, even if they did attract the attention of those in the house, would not be noticed until after the masked man had reached his destination. He made no effort to conceal his movements. Instead, he headed boldly for the building and moved close to the largest of the lighted windows. He could hear voices, and dropped under the window's edge to listen before making another move.

It happened that the Lone Ranger's arrival came at about the same time that Patricia was brought face to face with Bart Beldon. A quick glance through the window showed the masked man a strange scene. Beldon was tied to a chair, with Sam Slake's three henchmen watching him closely. The entire conversation could be easily overheard by the Lone Ranger. He recalled that Beldon had mentioned Luther Ponsonby, and he gathered also that Slake was mistaken in his belief that Beldon was in possession of evidence against the smugglers.

An understanding of the way the mind of a man like Beldon would function in such a situation made the Lone Ranger tense. He expected the government man to make some sort of break for freedom at any instant, and hoped the break would not come until Tonto had moved in closer with the horses.

Several times the Lone Ranger tried to catch Bart Beldon's eye and let him know that there was help at hand. Not until Beldon held the pad and pencil in his hand was the attempt successful.

Tonto's approach with the horses did not seem to be noticed by anyone inside the house. The Lone Ranger made quick gestures to the Indian, signs which only Tonto could interpret.

It was Mrs. Slake who brought things to a sudden head. Had she not happened to open the rear door of the house and catch sight of Tonto, the horses, and the masked man, the Lone Ranger might have waited longer and heard much more. This had been his hope. Beldon, knowing that the Lone Ranger was outside, would have been able to conduct a conversation with Sam Slake that might have brought out valuable information upon which to base plans for the future. Sam Slake's wife, however, seeing the masked man and Tonto, cried out in alarm.

Her shrill scream split the early morning. Before it had died away the Lone Ranger's hands dropped to his sides. He drew both guns, lashing at the window with one. Glass shattered into the dining room. Sam Slake turned with a curse. The masked man's gun barked and a silver slug crashed true to the mark. The knife leaped from Lefty's hand and flashed to one side as if by magic. The bullet had struck squarely on the gleaming blade.

Lefty stared, open-mouthed and unbelieving. Three men reached swiftly for their guns, while Sam Slake raced for a rifle that stood in the corner.

Again flame flashed from the Lone Ranger's weapons. One of the Slake men had his gun half out of the holster when a silver bullet struck it. The impact spun the gun in an arc across the room.

Then a tornado in the form of Tonto swept upon

the scene, crashing through another window in a shower of shattered glass. Tonto did not pause when his feet struck the floor. Head down, fists knotted, he charged into the first man he saw with a force that sent the smuggler sprawling to the floor.

There were yells without meaning, wild cries of fury, pain, and stark surprise. Sam Slake had his rifle at his shoulder by the time Bart Beldon himself got into the fracas. Beldon went into action with a chair. Swinging it over his shoulder, he threw it hard at Slake. One leg struck Slake in the forehead, and he dropped like a coyote that has run head on into a heavy-calibre bullet.

Tonto's fists were like battering rams, driving one after the other into the face of the huskiest man who still stood on his feet.

The Lone Ranger found that yells were futile in the clamor. He leaped across the windowsill, shot one arm about the waist of Patricia, and lifted the girl bodily out of the room.

"My horse," he shouted in her ear. "The white one! Go there and wait for me."

The girl nodded her comprehension.

When he saw that Slake and his three partners were momentarily out of the fight, Tonto grasped Beldon by the arm and gestured.

Beldon leaped through the window with speed that was amazing in a man of his size. He cleared the sill and sprawled on the ground. Tonto shouted something about a horse. Beldon looked where the Indian pointed and saw that his own horse, saddled, was there waiting. He leaped to the saddle.

The Lone Ranger swept Patricia to the back of his own big white stallion, while Tonto turned and threw several shots at the window in case anyone inside should show an inclination to pursue.

A cry rang out on the morning air, a cry that came just a split second before the thunder of hoofs.

"Hi-Yo Silver!"

It was a cry that thrilled both Patricia and Beldon as they heard it for the first time, a cry that filled them with fresh courage and made them feel that the bravery and goodness in *some* men went a long way to offset the evil and avarice in others.

"Hi-Yo Silver! Away!"

The Lone Ranger led the way, with Tonto and Bart Beldon close behind him.

"How strange!" thought Patricia. "I said he was the *one man* who couldn't be of help to me."

"Pony Horse," shouted Beldon to his mount, "I'm an addle-headed fool! That there is the man I *handcuffed* to keep him out of my way. *Now* look at him! Where in thunder would we be without him?"

Tonto grinned widely in the teeth of the rushing wind, and once more came the cry of the Lone Ranger:

"Hi-Yo Silver! Away-y-y!"

Chapter IX

PLAN OF CAMPAIGN

Patricia Knowlton's hair streamed and her skirt lashed and flapped in the wind that beat against her face. Talk was out of the question even though the girl was on the same horse as the Lone Ranger. She had to close her eyes and turn her face to the broad chest of the masked man who held her in front of him. Although he carried a double burden, Silver raced far in advance of the horses ridden by Tonto and Bart Beldon. It was a speed that no living creature could maintain for any length of time.

The Lone Ranger followed the course of the river, keeping in the open and scorning the shelter of the woods. He glanced back from time to time, wondering why none of Sam Slake's men came after him.

Several miles from the smugglers' headquarters, the masked man slowed down to a canter. Beldon and Tonto drew alongside. Then, at a slower pace, several more miles were put between the fugitives and the Slake ranch before the signal to halt was given.

The Lone Ranger dismounted, then helped Patricia to the ground.

"We'll rest the horses for a few minutes," he told Bart Beldon. "In the meantime you might unlock these handcuffs."

"Great Scott!" exclaimed Beldon, "have you been wearin' those things all this time? I forgot about 'em. How'd you bust the chain?"

"Tonto cut it."

Beldon drew a key from his vest pocket and removed the manacles. He shook his head slowly as he studied them.

"Must've took some fancy choppin'," he muttered.

He put the broken handcuffs in his hip pocket, looked at the Lone Ranger and scratched his cheek reflectively.

"There's a lot of things I don't understand," he said. "How did you get loose? Where did the Indian come from? How'd you happen to be at Slake's place just when you were needed?"

The Lone Ranger answered the questions as briefly as possible.

"There wasn't a chance," he added, "to get Miss Knowlton's horse from the corral. We were lucky to get yours in the time we had."

"I don't mind losing the horse," Patricia Knowlton said. "I'm terribly disappointed though. I was so sure that I could get the evidence that would hang all those murderers. I've been counting the days ever since they got Dad, waiting for the chance to square things."

The girl sighed heavily. She seemed to have no thought for her own safety. The fact that she had been rescued from almost certain death meant little to her. She looked at Bart Beldon.

"If only you hadn't blundered into Slake's place," she said.

Beldon looked with steady eyes at the girl.

"I reckon you must be mighty upset an' disappointed or you wouldn't say that. I didn't blunder into Slake's house. I went there with a well-planned scheme, an' took some good gunfighters with me. The whole trouble was this: Luther Ponsonby wasn't there."

"No, there wasn't anyone named Ponsonby there," affirmed Patricia.

"I took the men along, figurin' on raidin' the house, lettin' six-guns to the talkin' an' capturin' the gang. The plan was that Ponsonby would be captured along with the rest. When Ponsonby was captured, he was supposed to have all the evidence we needed. Then I found out that you were there."

"And?" queried Patricia.

"Well, I couldn't have a gun fight with *you* in the middle of things, so I had to concoct a scheme to get you out of the house first."

"But Ponsonby was *not* there."

"I didn't know that or I'd have changed the plans."

The Lone Ranger interrupted the conversation.

"I'd like to know more about Luther Ponsonby," the masked man said. "How did it happen that he was willing to help the law?"

Bart Beldon drew a huge blue handkerchief from his pocket and wiped the sweat and dust from his face. The Lone Ranger waited patiently for the law man to speak.

"I might as well tell you all there is to tell," said Beldon. "In the first place, you've got to understand how Slake keeps his men loyal to him. He's made every one of the crooks that work for him sign a full an' complete confession of everything he's done. Whenever one of the men get's a little hard to handle, Slake just reminds the gent that all he has to do is set the law on him an' turn over the confession of the man's crimes. There ain't a man workin' for Slake that don't have crimes enough against him to guarantee the hangman's rope."

"What would happen if Slake himself were to be captured?" asked the Lone Ranger.

"The men know that these confessions were kept for the law to find if anything happened to Sam Slake. That's why they're willin' to die fightin', if need be, to protect their boss. They might as well die fightin' for Slake, you see, because if Slake was to get caught, or killed, the rest of the bunch would hang."

"I understand," said the masked man.

"Well," continued Bart Beldon, "this man named Ponsonby did somethin' to make Slake sore at him. He felt that sooner or later Slake would have him put out of the way. Ponsonby let word out that he would help the law. He knew where Slake kept all those confessions as well as records and accounts that would hang Slake along with his men. The deal was this: Ponsonby would help me an' in return I'd burn the confession of Ponsonby's own misdoin's. That was fair enough to me. I was willin' to let one crook go free in order to get all the rest of 'em."

The Lone Ranger broke in.

"I heard some of the conversation when you were Slake's prisoner. You gave Slake the impression that Ponsonby had already turned the evidence over to you."

"Slake had the idea in the first place."

"He's sure of it now. He also has the idea that you'd destroy the evidence or give it back to him, to save the life of Patricia Knowlton."

"I wouldn't permit that!" said Patricia firmly.

"I was just stallin' for time when I said it," Bart Beldon explained.

"Slake doesn't know you were just stalling for time. All Slake will understand is that his own safety depends upon the recovery of the evidence. To recover the evidence he has to recapture Patricia and hold her as hostage. His move will be against the girl."

"Then I've got to get back beyond the Slake ranch an' get my men that are waitin' for me. We'll close in on Slake an' capture his gang."

The Lone Ranger shook his head.

"That won't do any good."

"Why not?"

"What would be your charges? In the eyes of the law, Slake's men are as honest as anyone. You've no proof of anything against them."

"I'd charge 'em with attempted murder!"

"You'd never make a jury believe charges like that. Slake would have a dozen witnesses against you."

Bart Beldon kicked angrily at a pebble.

"What in thunder should we do then?" he growled.

"First of all, take Patricia to town and keep her well guarded."

"But if I don't get back to my men, they'll think somethin's happened tuh me an' attack Slake's ranch."

64

"Tonto and I will go and tell your men to join you in Eagle Pass."

"By the time we get organized Slake'll have his men in hidin'."

"As long as they have to stay in hiding, their smuggling activities will be hampered. There's no use arresting them until we find Luther Ponsonby and get that evidence."

"I suppose you're right."

"Where are your men camped, Beldon?"

"About two miles the other side of the ranch. There's a place there where the woods go right to the edge of the river. That's where the boys are waitin' for me."

Beldon scribbled a brief note and handed it to the Lone Ranger.

"Show this to Dan Coffey. He's in charge of my men. It tells him that he's to do whatever you tell him."

The Lone Ranger tucked the message in his shirt pocket.

"Very well."

Chapter X

SMUGGLERS' ESCAPE

Slake was the last of the men in the ranch house to regain consciousness after the escape of the prisoners. He opened his eyes slowly and painfully. Disorder and confusion were on every side. The chairs and tables in the room were ruined and the men were nursing countless bruises.

Slake's head ached frightfully from the chair that Beldon had thrown, and it was several minutes before the leader could gather his wits and remember the details. He rose unsteadily to his feet and supported himself by leaning against the wall.

"Where'd they go?" he demanded without addressing anyone in particular.

It was Lefty who answered while he rubbed the hand that had held a knife until the Lone Ranger's bullet had disarmed him.

"Got away."

"I know that," snarled Slake. "Which way'd they go?"

"Headed toward Eagle Pass."

Slake spat contemptuously.

"A fine pack of weak sisters I got here," he said. "Why didn't some of you big strong so-called men stop 'em? What d'you think those shootin' irons are for?"

Lefty's eyes smouldered as he looked at the leader.

Slake continued raging at the men.

"With all of you that was here in the house, an' more in the barn an' bunkhouse, you let that masked man an' the Indian get away from here. I'd sooner have a couple of hound dogs to count on, than yellow-livered skunks like you!"

Lefty hunched his shoulders forward a bit and leaned toward Sam Slake.

"At any rate," he said slowly, "we stayed in the fight instead of takin' a nap on the floor in the corner."

"Meanin' *what?*" said Slake ominously.

"Meanin' that I think you played possom so's yuh wouldn't get yer precious hide shot up with the lead that was flyin'," retorted Lefty defiantly.

Slake took two steps forward and swung his open hand in a stinging slap on Lefty's cheek.

Caught off balance, the knife expert staggered to one side and clutched at the door to retain his footing. His hand darted instinctively for his gun. His fingers grasped the weapon's butt and froze there. Slake already held a gun and it was leveled at Lefty's eyes.

"Don't draw," said Sam Slake evenly.

The eyes of the two men met.

"I'm boss of this outfit," went on Slake. "While that's the case, I'm not takin' any lip from you. If any one don't like the way I run things, just say so an' we'll have it out."

He glanced from one to another of the men in the room.

The shortest of the men stepped forward and spoke in a mollifying voice.

"Now don't start shootin' it out, boys," said Shorty. "That won't git us nowheres." He turned to Slake. "Lefty's hand must hurt him somethin' fierce, boss. I seen it when the knife was shot away from him by the masked man." To Lefty, the speaker said: "The boss was really hit hard, Lefty. He ain't tuh blame fer feelin' that we let him down by lettin' them folks get intuh the clear."

After a moment, Slake put away his gun. Lefty turned and righted one of the chairs. He sat down and crossed his knees.

Arguments of this sort were not uncommon in Sam Slake's gang. The men were quick to flare up on the slightest provocation and were in the habit of settling their differences with six-guns. Living, as they did, under the constant strain and in the shadow of sudden death, their nerves were always raw.

Slake soused a cloth in a bucket of water nearby and held it against his bruised temple.

"One thing's got tuh be understood," he said. "I'm boss here."

Nods of agreement.

"We've got to light out of here an' go where it's safe until we can get that evidence away from Beldon. Now I've decided that the place to go is intuh Mexico. The Texas law can't touch us there."

"I reckon that's about all we can do," murmured Shorty.

"We'll make our headquarters there until we can capture that girl. Once we have our hands on her an' have her hid away, we can make some sort of deal with Beldon."

"I don't think the deal will be hard tuh make," one of the men said.

"That's the way I figure it. Beldon was all ready to make the deal when the masked man came in."

Sam Slake tossed the damp cloth into the water bucket and left it there.

"I want everyone in the outfit to be with us in Mexico. Shorty, you an' Dude saddle up an' ride north to the Indian country. You'll find the boys somewhere up there. They've only been gone for two days. Tell 'em to sell out what guns an' liquor they have, then join us in Mexico."

Shorty said: "Okay, boss. We'll be on our way."

"Lefty, you take charge of the packin'. Get what stuff we'll need an' load down the horses. We're pullin' out of here as fast as we can."

Lefty nodded and sauntered from the house.

Then Sam Slake called his wife from another room. He gave her a roll of paper money and told her to remain behind until he and his men had forded the Rio Grande.

"Then you go tuh the barn an' spill a lot of oil around the place an' set fire to it."

"Why, Sam?"

"The fire will destroy the stock of guns an' liquor we got hid in the barn."

"But what about me?"

"I'll leave a horse in the corral. As soon as you're sure the barn is burned to the ground, you ride north as far as Tall Pine. You know where my cabin is?"

"Yes."

"You wait there until I join you."

Accustomed to taking orders from her husband, the woman nodded. Her face expressed no emotion.

"I'll be there," she said.

Chapter XI

TONTO IGNORES A HUNCH

The Long Ranger and Tonto had followed the back trail until they were within a mile of Sam Slake's ranch. Then they had taken to the woods where the travel, though slower, was out of view of anyone on the ranch. Their plan was to reach Bart Beldon's men without being seen by the smugglers.

"We needn't have bothered about the woods," the masked man said when he and Tonto came within direct line of the ranch.

He pointed toward the far side of the Rio Grande.

"They've gone across the Rio Grande."

Tonto looked, shading his eyes with one hand. The distant horsemen were in water up to the bellies of their horses. Some had already reached the soil of Mexico.

"They didn't lose much time," the Lone Ranger said.

"Law not touch them now," said Tonto.

The Lone Ranger reined up.

"I'd like to investigate that ranch, Tonto," he said.

"Go there now?" queried the Indian.

The other shook his head.

"We should ride on to Beldon's men without further loss of time. I suppose we can stop at the ranch and have a look around the place after we've delivered Bart Beldon's message."

Tonto nodded, being in full accord with whatever the Lone Ranger decided to do.

"On the other hand, if Beldon's men pass that abandoned ranch, as they're sure to do on their way to Eagle Pass, they'll want to inspect the place."

"You not want um to do that?"

The white man looked uncertain.

"If I could only be sure that every one of Beldon's men was on the level it would be all right," he said. "But I'm not sure of that. There's a chance that Slake has one or two of Beldon's group on his own payroll. If that's the case, we'd have no chance of finding anything important while they were on hand."

"What we do?"

"Tonto, I can go on without you," the Lone Ranger decided. "You cut over there and look the ranch over. I'll go on with the message for the law men."

"What me hunt for?"

"Anything that might help us. Remember there are two things we must have. The first, and most important, is some sort of evidence against the smugglers. The second is a clue that will start us on the track of Luther Ponsonby."

Tonto signified his comprehension.

"Look for papers or records of any sort. If you find something, say nothing about it before the law men. I'll join you as soon as possible."

Tonto heeled the paint horse, swung the animal's

head toward the right, and cut from the woods. The Lone Ranger watched him for a moment, then continued toward Bart Beldon's men in camp.

Tonto approached the ranch at an angle that enabled him to see the corral beyond the buildings. It was a good thing he did. In the corral he saw a horse, fully saddled, tied to the rail. Though this might have been an animal that had been overlooked in the flurry of a hasty getaway, it might also mean that at least one man still remained inside the house.

Tonto was in plain view as he drew near the house. There was nothing to shelter him. He had to risk being seen and hope, if a shot were fired at him, the shot would go wild and give him the chance to fire once in return.

Nothing happened, however, as he reined up near the front porch, dismounted, and ascended the steps.

The front door stood invitingly open. Tonto advanced close to it and looked inside. He saw no sign of life. He was considering the advisability of entering boldly, when he heard the barking of a dog.

Wheeling quickly, the Indian turned toward the noise. The dog was a large beast with a shaggy coat of fur that was thickly matted with briars, brambles and caked mud. It stood on hind legs, clawing frantically at the barn door and giving every indication that it wanted desperately to enter that barn.

Tonto hurried to the dog.

"What matter?" he called in a friendly voice.

The dog dropped to four feet, barked, then wagged its plume-like tail in a way that was anything but antagonistic.

While the dog whimpered and nosed at Tonto's legs, the Indian examined the door of the big barn. He found it unlocked and opened it cautiously.

With a series of short barks, the dog leaped past the Indian, almost spilling him to the ground.

Tonto stepped through the door, then stepped quickly to one side and crouched in the shadows of the barn with his back against a wall. He waited there, tense and listening, for several moments while he let the pupils of his eyes adjust themselves to the gloom of the barn.

The dog, he saw, had gone directly to the far end of the building. He could hear the whines of the beast. Then there was more clawing of strong paws against wood. The dog, this time, was clawing at a section of the floor.

Tonto moved slowly and soundlessly toward the dog, still holding one hand close to the butt of his six-gun. His knowledge of animals served him in good stead. The dog, he knew, was after something that was beneath the boards of the barn floor. Tonto decided to investigate further.

When he reached the dog's side, he drew his gun and tapped the floor. A hollow sound gave indication of a basement or cellar of some sort. Inspection revealed a trap door that was fitted so cunningly that a chance visitor to the barn would never notice it.

The dog appeared quite willing to let Tonto experiment at opening the trap door. It stood back, head cocked to one side, ears pointing, and brown eyes fixed in a steady gaze that watched every move the Indian made.

Tonto ran his fingers along the barely perceptible crack of the closely fitted panel seeking for

74

something to grip. He found a knothole, hooked his finger into it, and lifted. He was surprised at the ease with which the door came up. He swung it all the way back, noting that it was fastened with well-oiled hinges.

Again the dog brushed past him. It dived, with a yelp, into the opening.

Tonto went below by means of a ladder, pausing when halfway down to reach up and close the door above his head.

He stood in the cellar of the barn on hard-packed dirt. Somewhere in the utter darkness, quite close at hand, he could hear the whining and breathing of the dog. There was something about the sound that gave him an uneasy feeling. He felt as if he stood quite close to something either dangerous or horrible, or both.

There wasn't time to waste in analyzing his impressions. He brought a short candle and matches from his pocket.

The candle, fixed upright on the ground, gave a feeble gleam that didn't reach the furthest portions of the cellar. Directly ahead of him, Tonto saw a row of wooden cases piled one on top of another until they reached almost to the rafters.

His uneasiness increased.

Tonto had the uncomfortable feeling that he was not alone in the cellar of the barn. It was a feeling that not only persisted, but grew stronger as the moments passed. He studied the wooden cases ahead of him, wondering if sudden death in the form of an outlaw with gun drawn crouched behind those cases.

In his tension, the Indian forgot the dog. He decided that he might as well precipitate action. He started toward the cases of contraband. After two steps he halted. Something peculiar in the dog's whine made him turn.

His eyes widened at the sight.

Not five feet from the candle, directly behind where he had stood a moment before, Tonto saw a man sprawled on the ground in a grotesque position. The man was on his back, eyes wide open in a fixed stare at the ceiling of the basement. His arms and legs were flung wide. The dog lay on its belly with its long nose touching the dead man's chest.

Tonto needed but a glance to know that the man had been dead for some time. He crouched beside the stranger, noting that he was at least as tall as the Lone Ranger, perhaps a little taller.

The cause of death was explained by a bullet wound in the left chest. Tonto subconsciously realized that a gun shot in the cellar of the barn would be muffled by the heavy planking of the floor above. It would scarcely be heard in the barn and certainly would not have been heard by anyone outside the barn.

The man did not look like the other members of Sam Slake's gang. It might have been death that softened his features. Whatever it was, the man's face was without the cruel lines and the unkempt appearance that characterized the smugglers Tonto had seen in the house a few hours previously.

Once more that uneasiness assailed the Indian. Surely the finding of the dead man could account for the previous "hunch" that there was something strange about the basement, but Tonto still felt apprehensive. His mistake was in ignoring the dictates of his sixth sense.

He felt in the stranger's pockets, looking for some

identification. Aside from a few coins and a crumpled package of tobacco, the pockets were empty. There was, however, something square and hard beneath the shirt.

Tonto reached in and found a leather wallet. He took this to the candle to examine it. He thrilled when he read the name that had been burned into the leather. It said "Luther Ponsonby."

Exictedly, Tonto opened the fat wallet and drew out some of the papers that made it bulge. He could hardly believe his good fortune. The hunt was ended, almost before it had begun. The wallet held evidence against Slake's gang!

Tonto's inspection of the papers was cut short by a sharp cry of pain from the dog. He turned in time to see the animal leap into the air, giving him a flashing view of wide jaws that held huge fangs. That was all he saw.

Something struck Tonto from behind. He was conscious of an instant of pain and a million, crazily dancing lights. He knew he was going down—knew unconsciousness was clutching him with an all-embracing grip. He fought against oblivion in vain.

A voice muttered in the candlelight, then a hand reached for the wallet and the papers. An instant later, a heel ground out the candle and the figure left the cellar.

Chapter XII

THE INFERNO

The angular form of Martha Slake paused at the door of the barn. The woman noticed that the latch was unfastened and mused that the men must have become careless in their hurry to get across the border.

She swung the large door wide and blocked it open with a rock.

"That'll give good draught," she reasoned. "Make the fire go faster."

She studied the direction of the wind and calculated that there was more than an even chance that sparks might set the house and other buildings on fire. Shrugging her shoulders in a gesture of indifference, she went inside.

Martha Slake hadn't always been a shapeless, unkempt woman. As she tackled the heavy tins of coal oil in the barn, spilling one after another over the barn floor, she continued the retrospective mood that had started on the second floor of the house. In packing her few things to take away with her, she had come across small souvenirs that had a sentimental value. Pressed flowers, an old school reader, tiny bits of faded ribbon that had once been bright and gay, and countless other things recalled a happier girlhood.

All this had taken time. Lost in memories, the woman hadn't seen Tonto's approach. Eyes that were a little misty hadn't noticed Tonto's horse when Martha Slake went from house to barn to carry out Sam's orders.

She opened the top of another can of oil, then pushed it on its side. The quick-burning liquid gurgled out to add to a rapidly spreading puddle on the floor. The cans were heavy, too heavy to lift. They were stored in the front part of the barn and it was there that Martha spilled the contents. She had no reason to go back toward the rear section where the trap door was located. Even if she had, it is doubtful that she would have noticed that the door had been recently opened. She was not observant at any time, and even less so now, in her reminiscent mood.

"Two more," she noticed.

The last of the oil spread out and soaked into the thirsty, dusty flooring. Then Martha Slake went outside. Going back to the rear door of the house, she secured a handful of oil-soaked rags, lighted them, and tossed them through the entrance to the barn.

Flames leaped up in a sheet, filling the wide door with a wall of fire. Wood that was like tinder caught and crackled.

Martha Slake turned her back on the inferno and headed for the horse that was packed and waiting to take her away. She hadn't the slightest suspicion that a dead white man and an unconscious Indian who would soon be dead, unless a miracle intervened, were beneath the floor of the blazing barn.

At the edge of the river a man looked back at the burning barn. He grinned in satisfaction, felt of a wallet that bulged with evidence against the Sam Slake gang, then rode toward Eagle Pass.

Scout, the paint horse, had hardly taken his eyes off the barn since Tonto had gone inside. The intelligent animal saw the flames and jerked away from the hitchrail. He dashed to the door, whinnied shrilly and tried to enter. The flames seemed to leap directly at his eyes. Stark panic filled the horse's heart but devotion to a master was an even stronger emotion.

He tried to dash through the flames. The first step of a hoof brought searing pain and an odor of burning hair that terrified the horse. He drew back, eyes wide and filled with fright—nostrils dilated.

Again the paint horse sounded an alarm and once more he tried to charge through the flames without success.

From somewhere overhead, a four-foot length of heavy wood dropped with a mass of sparks and flames and caught Scout on his arched neck.

He reared high, lashing with sharp fore-hoofs at an unseen attacker. He was confused, half-blinded, nearly choked with billowing smoke, and terribly afraid. Yet he tried again, and again, to reach the side of Tonto, his master.

Even his sense of hearing was assailed by the inferno. The flames roared and crackled with increasing fury. They had reached the roof at the front of the barn. Firebrands fell on every side, many of them striking the gallant horse.

Dazed and bewildered, Scout refused to retreat to safety. Yet he could not go ahead. Each effort to go through the flames brought new pain and added giddiness from inhaled smoke.

The cry of the Lone Ranger wasn't heard above the roar. Scout wasn't aware of the masked man's arrival until the mighty Silver raced close beside him.

"Take this horse away," cried the Lone Ranger.

Then there were other men on horses. One of these grabbed the reins that had been dragging on the ground. Scout fought instinctively against the pull that took him from the flames. He wanted to be with Tonto. If Tonto must perish, Scout, too, felt that he must die. He jerked and tugged, pawing furiously at the ground, digging sharp hoofs into the hard-packed dirt. It took the efforts of three men, in addition to the pushing of Silver on his side, to move Scout to safety.

"Tonto must be in there," the Lone Ranger shouted.

"You can't get to him," one of the men yelled back.

"I've got to."

"He's dead by this time. No man could live in a furnace like that."

"The fire seems to be concentrated in the front part of the barn," replied the Lone Ranger. "I'm going around to the side and back and see if there's another way to get in."

He raced Silver down the south side of the barn, pausing from time to time to look in at small windows while he stood in the stirrups.

The fire, he learned, hadn't reached the rear of the building.

"If Tonto is in the rear, he might still be alive," he thought.

But there was no way to get into the rear. He dashed across the back and up the north side of the big building.

"I've got to go through the flames," he told the men when he rejoined them.

"It can't be done."

"You sure your friend is inside there?"

"The floor'll cave in with the weight of a horse."

There were several other comments from Bart Beldon's men.

The Lone Ranger heard them while he hurriedly removed his neckerchief, soused it with water from his canteen, and tied it around the nostrils of his horse.

"Let me have your bandanna," he said, snatching the cloth from the man who stood nearest.

"Reckon you already got it," muttered the man.

The Lone Ranger blindfolded his horse.

Several tried to turn the masked man from his purpose. They argued that it was wanton waste of life to ride into the barn. "Even if you get in, you can't get out," they said.

"I'll handle this. Silver and I will get through somehow."

The men stood by their horses, futilely trying to do something about the flames and the man who might be dying in the barn. But there was nothing they could do.

The Lone Ranger guided Silver twenty yards away from the barn.

"It's up to us, old boy," he whispered. "You've got to run blind and depend on me."

Silver made no attempt to fight the blinding bandage or the cloth that protected his nostrils. He lunged ahead at the pressure of the rider's heel.

Straight at the barn, into the flames, charged the Lone Ranger with his head low, hugging Silver's neck. Then horse and rider were beyond the flames in a curdled fog of heavy smoke that made breathing almost impossible.

Silver was protected by the wet cloth but the masked man had no such protection. He leaped to the floor, tossing the reins over Silver's head. Jerking the reins, he cried, "Down, Silver."

Obediently the frightened horse dropped to the floor.

The masked man went to his stomach breathing the clearer air that was closest to the floor.

Hot smoke burned his throat and lungs. His eyes ached frightfully as he tried to peer about for some sign of Tonto. He called once, but his cry brought no response.

Then he heard faint cries from the men outside and looked over his shoulder. The sight was appalling. The floor, where the oil had been spilled near the door, had burned through. It had collapsed to leave a yawning hole between the horse and man and the outside.

There was no use wasting time or thought on this latest catstrophe. Tonto must be found first.

The Lone Ranger squirmed along the floor to the large boxes in one corner, thinking Tonto might be there. He felt the floor give slightly beneath his weight. He must have been guided by some kindly Fate when he paused to investigate the floor. Or it might have been a draught of cool air that came through cracks that demanded his attention. Whatever it was, the Lone Ranger found the trap door, opened it, and dropped below.

Close to the ladder, lighted by a red glow from above, he found the motionless form of Tonto.

A moment's investigation told him that Tonto was still alive. He breathed a word of gratitude as he lifted the heavy Indian to his broad shoulders and went up the ladder.

There was a one-in-a-thousand chance to escape.

The door was out of the question. Even though Silver could leap across the burned-through section, the Lone Ranger probably couldn't span the distance. He certainly could not cross it carrying Tonto, and Silver couldn't make the distance with a rider.

What windows there were had been made small intentionally by Sam Slake. The outlaw's desire to make them too small for a man to sneak through put them out of the Lone Ranger's consideration as a possible means of egress.

There was a one-in-a-thousand chance.

The Lone Ranger snatched the blindfold from his horse.

"It's up to you," he said.

He led Silver to the rear wall of the barn, lifted one of the forelegs and placed a silver-shod hoof against the wide planks that formed the siding.

"Go through," he yelled.

Silver seemed to understand. He reared, and came down with hoofs driving against the boards.

Again the white horse went to the attack. Splinters of wood flew from beneath the horse's hoofs. The wide planks split in several places.

"Again, Silver!"

Once more Silver tackled the assignment while the Lone Ranger gripped the shattered wood and tugged it away in long sections.

The opening was made. Fresh air and daylight streamed through.

Silver burst from the barn with a whinny of victory. The Lone Ranger followed an instant later, carrying Tonto in his arms.

Wild cries of praise came from Bart Beldon's men. They closed in on the Lone Ranger and Tonto, pouring rough, but nonetheless sincere, words of praise on a man and horse that had showed them a sight that would furnish food for conversation for many years to come.

Those hard-fighting law men admired sheer courage when they saw it. The demonstration by the Lone Ranger thrilled them as they had never before been thrilled.

They gave every aid they could. One man produced a first-aid kit and touched the places that were bruised or burned while others almost fought to have the honor of supplying water from their canteens.

The Lone Ranger's main concern was Tonto. He gave his friend a critical examination while the other men bathed the Indian's head.

In a few minutes Tonto opened his eyes. He had a dazed expression until he met the steady gaze of the Lone Ranger. Then a little smile of contentment spread from his lips to the rest of his face.

He said: "Tonto got plenty to tell."

Chapter XIII

THE TRAIL NORTH

"What happened to you?" "Who rapped your head?" "How'd the fire start?" "Who did it?" These were but a few of the barrage of questions that Bart Beldon's men threw at Tonto.

The Indian, however, remembered what the Lone Ranger had said. He shook his head slowly.

"Not talk now."

"We got a right to know what's been happenin' here," one of the Federal men declared.

The Lone Ranger said, "Beldon wants you men to join him in Eagle Pass at once. You've already lost a lot of time here. You'd better get going."

The men appeared reluctant.

"You have no choice. Beldon gave the orders. I simply passed them on to you."

"But he didn't know about the fire here."

"No. But he said for you to meet him and you'd better do it."

"Besides, we saw the horseman headin' away from the ranch, ridin' for the north like all-gitout."

The Lone Ranger, too, had seen the horseman, but the distance had been so great that it was impossible to tell who the rider was. The masked man didn't even know that it was a woman, not a man, who had left the Slake ranch in such a hurry.

"The most important thing at the present time is the life of Patricia Knowlton," the Lone Ranger said. "Some of you men may have known her father."

"I did," replied a Federal man. "Knowlton was one of the best."

"Slake's men," went on the Lone Ranger, "will be trying to capture the girl. Bart Beldon needs you at once to help guard her. Now get going. He'll tell you more about things that have happened here when you join him."

Finally the men mounted and started toward Eagle Pass.

Tonto found that he could stand without difficulty and was gratified to learn that his horse, Scout, had nothing worse than superficial burns.

While he smeared one of the wonderfully healing ointments of his own concoction on the horse's burns, the Indian told the highlights of what had happened. He was interrupted by the masked man.

"We'll get on the trail of the rider I saw when I came here."

"What rider look like?"

"I don't know, Tonto. It was too far to see much detail."

"Rider plenty important," said Tonto. "Me tell why."

The two swung to their saddles and headed into the woods. As they rode, Tonto explained his statement about the unknown rider's importance. He told of the finding of Luther Ponsonby, the wallet filled with evidence, and the blow from behind.

"Are you sure it was Luther Ponsonby's body?" asked the Lone Ranger.

Tonto nodded.

"But Sam Slake said that Ponsonby hadn't been around the ranch for at least two weeks."

"Me see Ponsonby in cellar."

"He could hardly have been there for the two weeks."

"Him dead mebbe two days."

"He must have returned, then, and been met by one of the men," the Lone Ranger said, as he tried to piece the facts together. "It's possible that there was a fight, unknown to Slake. Ponsonby was killed and his body hidden in the cellar. Then when the killer learned that Ponsonby had that evidence, he remained at the ranch while Slake and the others crossed the border. He went to get the evidence and heard you coming. So he hid and waited for a chance to knock you down. He took the wallet, set fire to the barn to hide what he had done, and rode away."

Tonto agreed that his assailant had been the one who had ridden into the woods.

The trail became obscure and further conversation was impossible. It was a trail that would have discouraged anyone but Tonto, and even he found it most difficult. Only in rare instances could a footmark of the horse be found. For the most part, the only clues were bits of horsehair that had been rubbed off by the rough trunks of trees, or freshly broken twigs.

As each sign was found, the Lone Ranger would remain at that spot while Tonto sought another telltale mark. Sometimes it took nearly an hour to find a single clue. Progress was painfully slow, and less than three miles had been covered when darkness made it necessary to postpone further trailing until morning.

The masked man and the Indian made camp. While the Lone Ranger unsaddled the horses and swung the saddles over the low branches of convenient trees, his friend prepared a small fire.

After a simple meal, the two rolled up in their blankets. Tonto seemed to go to sleep at once, but the Lone Ranger remained awake for some time, thinking.

He wondered if it might not be a waste of time to trail the fugitive. Surely that unknown rider must be far away by now. Yet, what else was there to do? The most important thing of all was the wallet of evidence that had been held by Luther Ponsonby. Without that, little could be done to jail the smugglers. With it, their conviction was assured.

Of course, there was no proof that the person who had knocked Tonto down had taken the wallet. It had been impossible to determine this. The wallet, and the evidence, might have been destroyed in the fire.

The masked man begrudged the time that had to be lost. He felt sure that the rider ahead would push on through the night and possibly increase the lead until it would be impossible to overtake him.

Yet, there was really no choice. To abandon the pursuit might mean the loss of the last chance to secure that evidence.

Finally the Lone Ranger slept.

Daybreak found him in the saddle.

The morning dragged by. Long intervals were spaced by short advances, sometimes less than ten yards at a time, as Tonto located sign after sign on the trail. It was plodding work, calling for great patience. There was a strong urge to assume that the rider ahead had held to a straight course and push on without stopping. But success could not be founded on assumption.

They broke from the northern edge of the woods at noon. The trail was visible then. The marks of a single horse stretched out ahead as far as the eye could see.

"Now," cried the masked man, "we can travel."

He nudged Silver with his heel. The great horse, apparently as impatient as its master, leaped ahead like an arrow from a bow. Tonto came right behind.

The rider, it seemed, had made no attempt to hide the trail. The course held to a straight line, constantly north.

At infrequent intervals the trail showed where there had been brief pauses at waterholes. Tonto examined the ground near each of these. It wasn't until the third stop in mid-afternoon that he found a footprint of the rider. He called the Lone Ranger to his side.

"Take look," he said, pointing.

It was an ordinary-looking footprint.

"What about it, Tonto?"

"You make mark alongside."

The Lone Ranger placed his booted foot next to the mark on the ground and made an impression. Then he saw the point. The mark of the rider ahead was only two thirds the size of his own.

"A small man," he said.

Tonto nodded.

"Maybe."

"What do you mean, Tonto?"

"No feller in Slake house small like that."

"There may have been men in the gang whom we didn't see."

The Indian shook his head dubiously.

"What is your idea, Tonto?"

"Feller hit Tonto on head."

"What has that to do with it?"

"Short man not hit top of head. Hit back of head instead."

"Do you think that the man we're following is *not* the one who knocked you out?"

Tonto expanded on his theory, explaining in words and grunts and gestures that a man small enough to make such a footprint would hardly be capable of overpowering Luther Ponsonby. This fact, or assumption, coupled with the fact that the Indian's attacker had struck the *top* of his head, made him fairly certain that there were two people involved—one whom they followed, another who had been in the cellar.

"At any rate," the Lone Ranger decided, "we've come this far. We're going to keep going until we overtake the person who rode away from that ranch."

Tonto mounted silently.

The copper-colored sun settled closer to the horizon on the left of the two who rode. For an hour there had been nothing said. The masked man and the Indian traveled side by side at the same ground-covering gait they had used all afternoon.

The land ahead was level, broken frequently by huge rocks that in some cases were fifteen or twenty feet in height. The shadows of these grew increasingly longer as the afternoon waned.

Suddenly Tonto signaled a halt.

"What is it, Tonto?" the Lone Ranger asked.

Without speaking, the Indian pointed ahead.

The trail went to the left of a mass of stone and stopped. The shadow of the rock stretched out on the ground, but that was not all. There was also the elongated shadow of a horse!

The trail was ended.

Chapter XIV

BACKTRAIL

Tonto headed for one side of the rock, the Lone Ranger for the other. The two were ready to fire at the first sign of a weapon raised against them.

Martha Slake stood with her back against the rock, her hands lifted shoulder high in a gesture of complete surrender. Her face was drawn by exhaustion and streaked with the dust of the trail. Her eyes were redened and dull.

"Don't shoot," she said in a colorless voice. "I ain't armed."

The Lone Ranger dismounted and stood before the woman.

"Put your hands down, Mrs. Slake, we're not going to shoot."

"I seen you comin' an' realized there wasn't a chance to get away from you. Now you've caught up with me, what are your plans?"

"You know, of course, that Tonto and I are friends of the people your husband held as prisoners?"

Martha Slake nodded.

"You know that we are trying to put Sam and all his men in prison?"

"I know."

"We're trying to find the evidence that Luther Ponsonby had."

"Beldon's already got that, ain't he?"

"No."

"I thought Beldon already had the confessions. He was ready to make a deal with Sam an' turn over all the evidence against the gang to save the life of that girl. That was when you busted intuh the house."

"Beldon gave Sam the wrong impression."

The Lone Ranger's voice took on a more friendly tone. He felt pity for this woman whose life had been filled with uncertainty and hardship. Though Sam Slake may have accumulated a fortune in illicit wealth, his wife had enjoyed none of the easy living or the luxuries that wealth could buy.

"Mrs. Slake, we know that Sam and his men have gone across the border where the law can't get at them."

"That's right."

"We also know that someone murdered Luther Ponsonby."

"Murdered him!" exclaimed the woman. "Where'd you find that out? When was he killed? Where?"

Her surprise was genuine.

"That double-crossin' polecat sure deserved killin' an' I'd like to shake the hand of the man that done it. Where'd you hear about it?"

"He was found dead in the cellar of the barn. Didn't you know about it?"

The woman shook her head.

"Do you know who set fire to the barn?"

"Sure! I did that myself. That was the last thing

Sam asked me to do an' I done it. I don't ever expect to see him again, so I figgered that I'd do what he wanted done."

"Why don't you expect to see him again?"

"Because I'm goin' home."

"Home?"

"All the way home. Sam told me to meet him—to wait for him north of here—but I'm not goin' to do it. I've thought about it a lot. I ain't stayed with that gang because I enjoyed it. I stayed because there wasn't anything else to do."

Martha Slake seemed eager to say more. It seemed as if she had been waiting for the chance to put into words the things that had simmered in her mind.

"If I'd tried to break away before this, Sam would have had me killed, the same way he's had others that knew things about him killed. Now I've got my chance I'm goin' to make the most of it. I'm goin' east as fast as I can get there."

The Lone Ranger nodded.

"You needn't think you can get me to help you capture Sam, though. He ain't been much of a husband to me an' there ain't no reason I should care, but I plan to shoot square with him. What you do to him ain't no concern of mine, as long as I don't help you do it. Do you savvy?"

"I understand, Mrs. Slake."

"Where'd you say Ponsonby was killed?"

"Tonto found him dead, in the cellar of the barn. The one who killed him probably stole the evidence against the gang. We hoped to get that evidence."

"You don't think I killed him?"

"No."

95

The Lone Ranger said nothing about how Tonto had been knocked down in the cellar of the barn.

"There was someone else on the ranch when you left."

"I thought I was the last tuh leave there."

"There must have been someone else. And while we stand here, that killer is getting away. We've got to get back to the ranch and find his trail."

"You ain't askin' no more questions?"

The Lone Ranger shook his head and mounted Silver.

"You ain't expectin' no more help from me? You ain't takin' me into Eagle Pass as a prisoner?"

"Can you ride as far as Tall Pine?"

"I can," replied Martha Slake.

"Go there and I think you'll find a stage that's heading east."

The woman nodded.

"Come, Tonto," called the Lone Ranger, "we've a lot of hard riding ahead of us."

In another instant the masked man and the Indian were heading south.

Martha Slake watched as long as she could see the departing men. It was hard for her, after so many years of association with outlaws, to understand the masked man who had treated her like a lady.

The Lone Ranger had to shout to make himself heard above the clatter of hoofs.

"There was nothing else to do, Tonto. We know that Martha Slake couldn't have been the one who knocked you down."

"That right."

"Therefore there must have been someone else at

the ranch, and we've got to find the trail of that man."

"Mebbe him cross river. Mebbe back with Slake gang by this time."

"If he's crossed the river," cried the Lone Ranger, "we'll cross after him. I'm going to have that evidence if I have to go all the way to Mexico City to get it."

Chapter XV

AN OUTLAW ALLIANCE

Lefty sat on a high branch in a tree near Eagle Pass. The dense foliage hid him effectively. A chance passerby could stand directly beneath the smuggler's lofty perch and not see Lefty. He had been there since daybreak and reckoned he had about one hour more to wait for darkness to make it safe for him to come down.

For the past several hours he had been fighting his better judgment. He wanted to get down, even though he knew the risk involved. His throat was parched and aching for want of water. He was ravenously hungry and his arms and legs were numb. The rope by which he had lashed himself to the main stem of the tree had worn raw places where it passed around his body. He was physically tired, having had no sleep for nearly two days. Lefty, in short, had suffered, and was suffering, untold discomfort.

He leaned to one side to get a glimpse of the sun settling beneath the horizon. " 'Bout an hour more," he muttered. "When I make 'em pay, they'll pay a-plenty fer all I had tuh go through."

It was Lefty who had murdered Luther Ponsonby.

The double-crossing member of the gang had walked to the ranch and met Lefty. There had been a quarrel and in the heat of battle Lefty had fired, killing the man who had stolen Sam Slake's personal papers.

Then Lefty, unaware of the important papers that Ponsonby had on his person, had dragged the dead man to the cellar of the barn. Later, the morning of the next day, when the story of the papers had been brought out by Slake and Beldon, Lefty realized what he had overlooked.

It had been a simple matter to lag until the rest of the smugglers were far ahead as they forded the Rio Grande, then return to search for the missing papers.

He had left the barn, after attacking Tonto, quite sure that Martha Slake had not seen him. He reached the river's edge, then paused. Behind him, the barn was in flames. He watched these for a moment, satisfied that all evidence in the cellar would be destroyed. He slapped his horse's rump, sending the beast across the river.

"Let 'em all wonder what's happened tuh me," he muttered. "It'll be best if there ain't no horse's tracks headin' fer town."

He started for Eagle Pass on foot. At one point he heard the hoofbeats of approaching horses and ducked behind convenient rocks.

Bart Beldon's men passed within fifty feet of Lefty. He was fortunate indeed to have found the rock to shield him. He realized that he would have no chance at all to barter for his life if he were captured with the documentary evidence in his possession. He decided to play safe. Instead of going on toward Eagle Pass and running the risk of being overtaken by other law men, he would remain in hiding until darkness came.

The afternoon dragged on. Lefty studied the evidence and noted that there was a confession for each member of the gang, with one exception. Luther Ponsonby, apparently, had destroyed his own confession. Lefty selected the paper which had his own name signed at the bottom. As he read it, he mumbled curses at Sam Slake and the method by which the leader had held him in the gang.

He touched a match to the confession and watched it burn to black ash. He crumbled the ashes to powder and let the breeze carry the powder away.

He tried to sleep, but the sun was blistering hot and there was no shelter. He counted the seconds until they were minutes, and marked the minutes until these stretched into an hour. He became hungry, but there was no food. He was thirsty, but he didn't dare cross the open stretch to reach the muddy water of the Rio Grande. He bided his time, finding some small satisfaction in contemplating the manner in which he would be repaid.

When darkness came, Lefty set out, following the river, toward Eagle Pass. His feet in high-heeled boots were soon blistered, and his legs, unaccustomed to walking more than a short distance, were tired and aching. He wondered if he had been wise to send his horse away. Pushing on, with frequent halts to rest, he winced with the pains that shot from heel to hip at every stride.

His progress was slow and it was dawn before he came in sight of town. Then a new complication arose. He had counted on the help of Baldy Brennen, clerk in the Eagle Pass hotel, but he couldn't reach Baldy at daybreak. As a matter of fact, he couldn't be sure of finding Baldy at the hotel desk until evening. This meant that he had an entire day ahead of him which must be spent in hiding.

There were too many Federal men in town to risk exposure in search of Baldy. He had no choice. He had to hide someplace until evening. But where was there to hide? It was open country without a hill or cave, or gully of any sort. Lefty paused beneath a huge tree to consider things. He noticed the tree itself—the density of the foliage, and decided that this must be his hiding place.

With some difficulty he finally succeeded in climbing the rough trunk of the tree to the lowest branch. Then it was a simple matter to climb higher. He found a branch that served his purpose, settled himself upon it and tied himself to the tree. At first it was a relief to sit down, even on the uncomfortable branch. In less than an hour he regretted his choice of a hiding place, but it was then too late to make a change.

People were coming and going between town and the surrounding ranches at irregular intervals. Lefty didn't know how well known he was in the community, but true to his determination, he decided to play safe and stay where he was in spite of the discomfort.

As the afternoon advanced, he sank into something like a stupor, waking when his weight was thrown against the ropes that bound him. It was one of the longest days in the outlaw's life, but he kept telling himself that he'd be paid—paid plenty, and ultimately sunset came. Then dusk. Darkness.

Lefty's fingers were too numb to tackle the knots in the rope. He drew a knife and cut himself free. He started to climb down and was amazed at the refusal of arm and leg muscles to obey the commands of a bewildered brain. He fell to the ground and lay there for some time. Then he kneaded his muscles and restored the circulation. Finally he could stand.

"Now," he growled, "I'm headin' fer town. Soon as I see Baldy Brennen, I'll get some grub. Then I'll feel a sight better. Me an' Baldy can handle things so's we'll both get rich."

Like a furtive beast, he headed for town, but avoided the street that ran between two rows of buildings. He noticed that a number of men were about, more than were usually to be seen in Eagle Pass. He turned to his left and went behind the row of buildings until he came to one that was taller than the others.

The two-story hotel in Eagle Pass boasted no less than a dozen rooms in which guests could be accommodated. Four of these were in the rear of the first floor, the others on the floor above. The front part was given over to a sort of lobby and office on one side and a bar on the other.

Lefty crept along the side of the building on which the office was located. He came to a window and peered inside. His evil features relaxed when he saw the man who sat behind the desk.

Baldy Brennen was short, fat, and as innocent of hair as his name implied. His eyes were set in pouches of flesh and his cheeks hung flabbily and wobbled in a jelly-like way when he moved. His complexion was neither red, like that of many overweight men, nor tanned, like that of most men who lived in Texas. It was pasty-white, like something that lived beneath a rotting log.

Baldy sat on one chair with his feet on another. He leaned back with his eyes half closed and his pudgy hands clasped across a vest that was unbuttoned and connected only by a heavy, gold watch chain.

He thought he heard someone whisper his name and looked up to find the lobby of the hotel empty. He had just closed his eyes when he once more heard someone say "Baldy." Instinct made him turn toward the window. He saw Lefty.

"You," he said, wide-eyed in surprise.

He hurried to the window.

"Get away from here, Lefty. Get out of town an' be fast about it. Anyplace else in the hull of the world would be more healthy than Eagle Pass fer you."

"Shut up," commanded Lefty in a low, tense voice. "I'm here an' I aim tuh stay here. Is it safe for me tuh come through the window? Is there anyone about?"

"'T ain't safe for you to come through the window now, or any other time. Bart Beldon is in town an' he's got every man that's able tuh tote a gun swore in to help him. What you doin' here anyhow? Where is Slake an' the rest of the bunch?"

"In Mexico I reckon."

"What you doin' here then? Why ain't you with the rest of the gang?"

"I can't stand here with my chin perched on the windowsill an' palaver all night with you, Baldy. I got plenty to say an' plenty to do, but I've got tuh have a place tuh hide in an' some food to eat. I've had a tough time gettin' here."

"Looks that way."

Baldy glanced behind him furtively and then looked toward the door.

"How long you got tuh stay here?"

"I don't know."

"Is it the true fact that Slake tried tuh murder Knowlton's daughter?"

"Is that what's bein' told around town?"

"It is."

"I reckon Slake might've killed the girl, if he'd had tuh do it."

"Has Sam lost his head all of a sudden? Everyone knows that it was Slake that dry-gulched her old man, but they're willin' tuh let that pass, bein' as Knowlton was a law man an' slated tuh get shot sooner or later anyway. But with the girl it's different. Slake can't threaten *her* an' get away with it."

Lefty's nerves were stretched to the braking point. He lost patience with the long-winded hotel clerk. A gun appeared in his hand.

"Stop stallin', Baldy."

Baldy's eyes popped wide.

"Put the shootin' iron down, Lefty," he said. "There ain't no call for you to hold a gun on me."

"I'm takin' no chances. Now show me to a room where I can hide for a time, or I'll start shootin'."

"I was only tryin' to tell you, Lefty," said the fat man apologetically. "The folks in Eagle Pass are down right sore at the way the Knowlton girl was held. Course there's nothin' could be *proved* in court, but all the same—"

Lefty was through the window and at Baldy's side. He nudged the other with his gun and said, "Get goin'."

Baldy nodded, rose from his chair, and waddled down the corridor with Lefty close behind him.

"I'm on your side, Lefty, the same as I've always been. I'm only tryin' to tell you that this town ain't safe for you."

Lefty made no comment. He noted with satisfaction that the hall was uncarpeted and would make audible the footfalls of anyone who approached the room he was to occupy.

Baldy opened the last door on the left side.

"You'll be all right in here," he said. "You've got one window on the side an' one on the back."

"Good enough," said Lefty, stepping into the room. "You come in here when you've got time to talk," he told Baldy. "I'll tell you how we can both get rich."

Baldy struck a match and lighted a lamp on the dresser.

"I don't understand why you're here without Sam," he said, replacing the chimney. "Ain't you an' him workin' together no more?"

"Nope. I'm on my own now, Baldy. I'm takin' you in as my partner."

Baldy nodded.

"It's all right with me, providin' there's money in it without no risk."

"There's money in it all right."

"Risk?"

"Not much. In fact, none at all, unless we muddle things."

"Where's the money comin' from?"

"I've got the details pretty well worked out," said Lefty. "I plan to collect in two ways. I've got somethin' here," he tapped his shirt, "that Bart Beldon would pay plenty to have. I know where to get somethin' that Sam Slake would give a heap of cash to get his hands on."

"What's under yer shirt?"

"Tell you when you can sit down an' talk things over with me."

Baldy Brennen nodded.

"I'll be in tuh see you," he said, "as soon as I get a chance."

Chapter XVI

SLAKE'S RETURN

Sam Slake had not achieved his position of leadership by reticence or cowardice. In addition to courage, he had another quality that made him a natural leader. He knew when to retreat.

He had deemed it wise to take his men across the border where they would be secure for the time being. That, however, did not mean that he intended to keep them there. Far from it. Slake's plans called for the capture of Patricia Knowlton and as soon as possible he would open his campaign toward that objective.

In Mexico, Slake had a great advantage. He was unhampered by law and could therefore fight wherever it was most convenient. The Federal men, on the other hand, had no authority below the border.

When the smugglers arrived at a campsite in the hills a few miles from the Rio Grande, Lefty's absence was noted. For the time being, however, little attention was paid to this. There were many details that occupied the men's attention. The camp had to be settled, horses staked to graze, food prepared and sleeping arrangements made.

Slake appointed men to serve as guards and stationed them at intervals along the trail between the camp and the river. Then, after dark, he rode as far as the water's edge and looked at his ranch. The barn, what was left of it, glowed redly as the embers smouldered. The house appeared unharmed by the fire, as did the bunk house. There was no sign of life about the property. In the light of the moon he could see that the horse which he had left in the corral was gone.

When he turned in for the night, Sam Slake lay awake for some time contemplating what he would do. The first and most important task was to capture Patricia Knowlton. Convinced, as he was, that Bart Beldon held evidence against his gang, Slake felt that he could secure that evidence, if only he could kidnap the girl. The girl must be in Eagle Pass. The conclusion, then, was that a group must go to Eagle Pass and get her. Disguised? Perhaps that would be the safest way. For half an hour Sam Slake thought of various forms of disguise that might be used. Then he slept.

The next day he rode twenty miles deeper into Mexico. He met and conferred with some of his friends and made sure that Mexico was safe for him. He had thought it would be; had always been careful, in fact, to violate no laws in that country, but he wanted to be sure.

During the solitary ride back to his camp, Slake thought of Lefty. For the first time since crossing the border, the leader of the outlaws devoted his mind to the missing member of the gang.

"Doggoned odd," he mused. "His horse came over with us. Lefty couldn't o' drowned in the river. 'T ain't deep enough. There wasn't any gunplay, so he couldn't o' been hurt. Must be that he stayed back on purpose. Now why in thunder did he do that?"

He tried to apply his customary logic in understanding Lefty's desertion. Lefty couldn't travel far without a horse. Lefty wouldn't, even if he could.

Pondering on Lefty's recent actions, Slake decided that the knife expert had, for some time, wanted to be free of the gang. Now that Slake no longer held the evidence that would send him to jail, there was no reason to remain loyal. Slake could readily understand that part of it. Yet, why had Lefty sent his horse with the gang?

"Perhaps," muttered Sam Slake, "he figured the horse was pretty well known to all of our boys an' he didn't want the critter to be spotted by us. On the other hand, he *had* tuh have a horse."

Suddenly Sam exclaimed, "By Juniper!"

He dug his spurs deep and his horse, frightened by the savage attack, leaped ahead and raced the rest of the way to camp.

Slake's horse slid to a halt and the rider leaped from the saddle, shouting.

"Boys, all of you! Come here! Come quick!"

The smugglers, some of them snatching guns, ran to their leader like iron filings leaping at a charged magnet.

"What's the matter, boss?"

"What's up?"

"The law after us here?"

"*Shut up!*"

The last command came from Slake.

"Let me talk! You boys listen, an' listen sharp."

The men were silent, but tense.

109

Slake named the two men who were toughest and strongest.

"Bull! Trigger! You two get a brace of guns an' plenty of cartridges. Bring rifles too. Saddle up the best horses in the outfit an' get ready to ride with me. We're goin' after Lefty."

"What's he done?" asked Jones.

"Cleared out."

"But, boss, what's to be gained by goin' after him?"

Jones, a friend of Sam Slake for many years, was the only one of the gang who could question the leader without arousing Slake's anger.

"I was thinkin'," said Slake. "Thinkin' about Lefty an' the fact that his horse came here with us. Then it struck me why he didn't need his horse."

"Why?"

"He took the horse I left in the corral for Martha."

Jones pursed his lips and looked thoughtful.

Slake yelled, "You—Bull, Trigger—hurry up. The rest of you men get ready to ride too. We're all goin' out."

Then Jones spoke again.

"Now look, boss, I know that you've already got your mind made up . . ."

"I have!"

". . . an' it ain't for me to try an' change it, but I still don't savvy why it makes so all-fired much difference *what* horse Lefty took. He ain't here an' that's all there is to it."

"If he took Martha's horse, she wouldn't be able to leave the ranch, would she?"

"I reckon not."

"If she was stuck at the ranch, she might think I

was tuh blame for it. She might get the notion that I'd left her there without a horse, on purpose. Then she'd be mad. Mighty mad at me. She'd likely do all she could to get square."

"But," said Jones, "what could she do?"

"Sooner or later the Federal men will show up at the ranch, huntin' for clues. She'll tell 'em all she knows about us."

"She couldn't give no proof that would stand in a court o' law, though."

"I'm not takin' chances," retorted Sam Slake.

Bull and Trigger rode up to the boss's side on powerful horses and signified by nods that they were ready.

Slake instructed the rest of the men to follow as far as the edge of the Rio Grande, and wait there.

"If you see me an' the other two in trouble, then you're to cross the river an' help us. But if there's no shootin', stay on this side of the water. You all got that straight?"

Slake looked from one to another of his men and saw their nods.

"All right then. Let's get goin'."

Instead of crossing the river at the point nearest the ranch, the party moved a few hundred yards upstream to ford the river at a point that could not be seen from the ranch.

The crossing itself was uneventful. On the Texas side, Sam Slake dismounted. Bull and Trigger followed suit. The trio made its way toward the ranch, crouching low, and with guns in readiness.

The sun had gone down and in another few minutes it would be dark.

Slake suddenly raised a hand and halted.

111

"Look," he whispered hoarsely. "Someone is around the buildings."

Bull looked over Slake's shoulder. He saw forms moving in the dusk—saw two horses disappearing beyond the house.

Trigger was about to speak, but Slake silenced him with a gesture.

"You, Trigger, get back to the horses, keep 'em quiet while me an' Bull go closer to them two."

Trigger nodded and retreated.

Slake dropped to the ground, Bull at his side. Together the pair snaked closer to the buildings on their bellies. They took advantage of tall grass and weeds, keeping as much out of sight as possible until they reached a point where the two ahead of them were concealed by the ranch house. Then Slake rose, and ran ahead.

"When we get to the house, we'll slip inside," he said to Bull.

"Whatever you say, boss. Who are those two *hombres?*"

"I got an idea, but I ain't sure yet."

"What're they doin'?"

"Dunno," said Sam Slake shortly.

They reached the house and crept inside.

It was quite dark in the ranch house but Sam Slake knew where every article of furniture was placed. He made his way to the window nearest the last position of the intruders and was gratified to learn that it was open. He peered out and saw a tall white man whose face was masked, and an Indian.

Slake's grin when he spoke was an evil thing to see.

"The Lone Ranger an' Tonto. I got a score to settle with them two."

Bull nodded.

"I'll settle it for you," he muttered, drawing his six-gun.

"Not that," whispered Sam Slake. "A six-gun might miss 'em. Use your rifle."

"Suits me."

Slake cocked his own rifle, throwing a cartridge into firing position. Both men rested their weapons on the windowsill.

"I'll cover the masked man," Slake said. "You draw a bead on the redskin an' be sure the first shot gets him in the heart. Then get his buddy."

Slake never did his own killing.

"I never miss," stated Bull.

"Hold your fire just a minute though. I want to know what those two are doin'."

Slake watched the masked man and Tonto studying the ground between the house and the river's edge. They seemed to be looking for something, perhaps tracks. They bent to hands and knees, sometimes lighting matches and holding them within six inches of the packed dirt that had been washed smooth by the rain.

The voice of the Lone Ranger, calling to Tonto, reached Sam Slake's ears.

"Here, Tonto," the masked man said. "Here's the track we're looking for."

Tonto hurried to the side of the Lone Ranger.

"Give 'em a couple more minutes," murmured Sam Slake. "We'll see what they're huntin' for."

The masked man's voice came again.

"Here's where he came ashore on foot. It must have been one of the gang who started out with the rest, then left his horse and came back."

"He's found Lefty's tracks," thought Slake.

113

"Him," said Tonto, "wear-um high-heel boot."

"That's right, Tonto, and he started walking toward Eagle Pass. Now we have the whole story. He left his horse and came ashore. We found his tracks leading to the barn, then coming away from the barn and following the water toward town. Now," the Lone Ranger rose to his feet, "we have the man we want. We'll follow him."

"You heard him?" asked Slake.

Bull nodded.

"They've found Lefty's trail. They're goin' to follow it."

"Yeah, that's what I figgered, boss."

Slake put his thumb on the hammer of his rifle and gently lowered it. "We'll let 'em live fer a while."

Bull said, "I'll go tell Trigger."

"Wait."

"Yeah?"

"Tell Trigger to go back an' join the rest of the bunch. Tell 'em that you an' me are goin' to follow Lefty's trail, lettin' the Lone Ranger pick it out fer us."

"You ain't goin' to let the Lone Ranger get away?"

"Of course not, but as long as he's so doggoned good at followin' a trail, we'll let him follow Lefty's. All we got to do is follow the Lone Ranger an' he'll lead us to Lefty."

"Sure thing."

"You can put a bullet in him any time I say. Now go send Trigger back to the rest of the outfit. The boys are to pack everything and move along the Mexico side of the river. They can camp across the

114

river from Eagle Pass. Then they'll be on hand when they're wanted."

"I'll tell Trigger."

"I figured we'd have to get near Eagle Pass anyway; that's where the girl is."

"Seems like we're goin' to a lot of trouble just to locate Lefty," said Bull.

"There might be more reason than we think tuh locate him. That critter must've had some reason for headin' into Eagle Pass on foot. He wouldn't walk that far unless there was somethin' mighty important tuh walk for."

Bull nodded and left.

Chapter XVII

CAPTURE

Silver pawed the ground and showed other signs of uneasiness. After a moment, Scout also went through familiar motions that had always meant a warning of danger or intruders close at hand. The Lone Ranger edged close to Tonto's side while he continued to study the ground.

"Quiet, Silver, we'll feed you pretty soon," he called in a loud voice.

Then he spoke very softly to Tonto.

"There's someone near us, probably watching. Listen for any sound."

Tonto nodded.

"Hear sound short time back," he whispered. "Me think men come this side of river."

"What else did you hear?"

"Hear rifle cocked."

The masked man felt a sensation of prickling needles in his back. Instinctively he felt that guns were steadied on him, yet he gave no outward sign. A sudden move might cause the one who held the gun to fire. He must use every precaution. He dared not look behind him, toward the house, even though he felt sure he'd see the man who had the drop on him.

He reached in the pocket of his shirt and drew out a bit of glass.

"Sometimes," he said in a normally loud voice which he knew would be heard by anyone in the house, "a footprint can be seen better through a magnifying glass."

He took out a glass, which was not a magnifying glass as he'd hinted, but a small hand mirror that he used when disguising himself, and held it in such a way that he could see the reflection of the house. The last of the diminishing daylight, fell across the west side of the house in a rosy, sunset glow. He saw the window, which was open, and the head and shoulders of Sam Slake.

"Give him some reason to postpone shooting us," he thought, quite unaware that Slake already had postponed the execution.

"Tonto, now we know where we're going."

"That good," replied the Indian catching the cue and speaking loudly.

"When we reach the end of this trail, we'll have the evidence against Sam Slake's gang. Slake doesn't know that Beldon has *not* got the evidence. Slake won't dare come on this side of the border. We'll get the confessions, then find a way to trap Sam Slake into crossing the river."

Slake, hearing every work distinctly, grinned in satisfaction.

A number of details were cleared up in Sam Slake's mind when he heard what the masked man said. So Beldon did not have the evidence after all. It was Lefty who had it, and Lefty had gone toward Eagle Pass.

"The original scheme can stand," thought Slake. "We'll follow the Lone Ranger until he locates Lefty an' gets that evidence, then we'll open fire!"

He cursed Lefty, and silently vowed that he would make sure the former member of the gang paid in full for the double-cross. He asked himself how it happened that Lefty, not Ponsonby, had the confessions, but decided that explanations would come in the course of events.

The Lone Ranger and Tonto mounted their horses and started off at a brisk trot.

The moon, when it rose, was favorable. Following Lefty's footprints was a simple matter. The Lone Ranger and Tonto observed where he had paused to wait while Beldon's men rode past; then saw several places where he had stopped to rest.

It was fortunate that Lefty had kept closer to the water than the Federal horsemen. Otherwise his tracks might have been obliterated.

From time to time, as he rode, the masked man drew the mirror from his pocket and looked over his shoulder. By the light of the moon he could easily see the two who followed him. Slake and Bull were making no effort to lessen the gap. They seemed content to remain about two hundred yards behind. To make sure of this, the Lone Ranger halted once to give the horses a chance to drink. The others also halted and drew back in the shadows of a clump of trees.

"They're staying right with us," the Lone Ranger told Tonto grimly. "Slake's counting on getting the evidence."

Tonto nodded.

"What we do?"

"We'll keep on until we're near Eagle Pass. Then we'll take care of those two crooks."

Tonto grinned knowingly.

"I don't intend to let them take a shot at us if we can help it. The surest way to prevent that is to capture them. If we can just locate the man we're after, I have a scheme that I think will work out."

"That good."

"It may not be easy to find the man we want though. I'm sure it's a member of Slake's gang, but that's about all we know about him."

The masked man and Tonto continued on the trail.

"Where," inquired the Indian, "we look first?"

The Lone Ranger shook his head and rode for the next ten minutes in silence. He asked himself where the man who had the evidence would be most likely to go. To what use would he put that evidence? Surely he didn't intend to hand it to Sam Slake, or he would not have gone to Eagle Pass. To Beldon then? That was quite possible. Luther Ponsonby had wanted to give the evidence to the Federal man. Perhaps the man who killed Luther Ponsonby would try to negotiate a deal.

At any rate, Bart Beldon was the logical one to call on first.

There remained the menace of Sam Slake and his companion.

The Lone Ranger slowed as he approached a tall tree that stood apart from any other growth. The trunk was a full three feet in diameter, plenty thick enough to offer concealment. With a word to Tonto, he dropped lightly to his feet, his rope in hand.

"Keep going, Silver," he called.

He stepped behind the tree that had been Lefty's roosting place until about three hours ago, and shook the loops of his rope free, forming a huge noose.

He waited, listening. Hoofbeats drew nearer. Then he heard Slake speak to the rider next to him.

"We'll risk followin' 'em right intuh town, Bull, we can't take a chance on losin'—"

Sam Slake's speech ended in a choking gasp of surprise.

The Lone Ranger moved with lightning speed. He gave a sudden tug on his end of the rope. The noose jerked tight, hauling Slake and Bull into a close embrace and spilling both to the ground.

Violent howls of rage and livid curses filled the air. Slake fought desperately to get his gun out of the holster. He had it half drawn when the masked man stepped close.

"Don't move!"

It was a command, backed up by two guns which were held steadily by the masked man.

"If you finish your draw, Slake, I'll blast the gun from your hand."

"Tricked!" snarled Sam Slake.

"There are a lot of things you'll find it hard to understand, Slake. This may be one of them."

"The law ain't got nothin' ag'in me," Slake said in a surly voice. "I know the truth o' things now. Beldon ain't a shred of proof against me. All that was said the other day, about him havin' evidence, was lies."

"Not lies, Slake, just a misunderstanding on your part. You took too much for granted."

"What're you figurin' to do with us, now that you got us?"

"Nothing."

Slake looked surprised at this.

"Nothin'?" he echoed.

"I'm going to fix you so you'll keep out of trouble and be around when I want you again."

Tonto rode up and dismounted.

"Get ropes on Slake, Tonto," said the Lone Ranger. "I'll take care of his friend."

The Indian nodded and went about his task with a deftness that showed long practice. He tossed a rope about Slake's ankles and drew a tight loop. Then he brought the rope to Slake's knees, passed it twice around and knotted it. The long end was then brought up higher on the man's back and his wrists were trussed, one across the other. The remainder of the rope was coiled about the captive's chest and biceps, binding his arms close to his body.

Meanwhile, the Lone Ranger performed a similar operation on big Bull. Fortunately they were out of sight of the men on the other side of the river.

When he finished, the Lone Ranger rose to his feet and addressed Sam Slake.

"You'll have a hard time understanding the things I do, Slake. You'll be better off if you don't even *try* to understand them."

Slake glared at the masked man without replying.

The Lone Ranger went on.

"I'm going to leave Tonto here to watch you two. I expect to be back here before daybreak and I might bring something you're very anxious to have. If I fail, Tonto will know what to do."

Tonto nodded without speaking.

"One thing more, Slake," said the Lone Ranger as

he prepared to mount his horse. "Do you know which member of your gang sent his horse across the river without him?"

"What if I do?"

"Who is it?"

"None of your business."

"But I am making it my business. I'll find him in Eagle Pass, whether you tell me or not. If you *do* tell me who it is, I'll find him that much sooner. The sooner I find the man, the sooner I'll be back here."

"What are you figurin' to do with us when you get back?"

"You'll have to wait and find out. I'll promise you one thing, however."

Slake showed interest.

"You'll be mighty uncomfortable in about an hour and you'll be wishing you were free of those ropes. I can probably be back here in an hour, if I don't have to spend half the night looking for one of your men in town. Do you want to name the man, or stay here all night?"

Bull broke in.

"I'm uncomfortable already, boss, what's the difference if we tell him or not? Let him know who tuh hunt for."

Slake strained against the rope and found that the masked man had spoken the truth. He could barely move a muscle and, in a very short time, he would be in misery.

"I'll tell you," he grumbled. "It was Lefty."

"Lefty?"

"You saw him in my place. He's the lean, hungry-looking critter that likes knives."

"I remember him."

"Now suppose you tell me a few things that I hanker to know."

"What, for example?"

"Where is Luther Ponsonby? How'd Lefty get the evidence away from him?"

"Ponsonby was murdered."

"By Lefty?"

The masked man nodded in the affirmative.

"I think so," he said.

"Where at?"

"I don't know much more about it, Slake. Tonto found Ponsonby dead, in the cellar of your barn. Now I am going on to Eagle Pass. I have some important things to take care of."

"*Wait!*"

Slake's voice held a tone that was almost a plea.

"What do you want?" the Lone Ranger asked.

"Why're you treatin' me friendly, sort of. Just what is your game?"

Without replying, the masked man mounted and rode away.

Chapter XVIII

BALDY MAKES A PROPOSITION

Bart Beldon sat in the comfortable living room, talking to Patricia Knowlton. The girl, at the Federal man's insistence, was staying at the home of his sister, who was away on a visit.

"It's about time for me to turn in," Patricia said, looking at a clock on the mantel over the fireplace.

"Reckon so," returned the Federal man. "Fact is, it's later'n most folks stay up. Most eleven o'clock."

"You needn't worry about guarding me, Mr. Beldon," said Patricia. "I'm not at all afraid to stay here."

Beldon rose.

"I have a gun," Patricia continued. "I'll keep it right beneath my pillow. I'm not afraid to use it either, so don't have a moment's concern about me. As a matter of fact, I wish some of those crooks *would* come here. I think I'd like a chance to shoot them."

There was a trace of a grin on the hard features of the big Federal man.

"Won't be no need for you to handle a shootin' iron," he said. "I've got my men all around the house."

"That makes me feel like a prisoner."

"I'm downright sorry," Bart Beldon said evenly. "The point is, though, we can't take no chances. Slake has the notion that he can get back the evidence against his men if he captures you. He'll make a play to do that sooner or later."

"But your men told you that Slake's gang had crossed the border."

"That don't fool me none. He'll make his headquarters where we can't get at him, but he'll be around. Don't you worry, though. I have given my men orders to be on watch an' they'll stay on the job."

Patricia sighed. "Prisoner," she murmured.

Beldon said "Good night" and turned to leave.

Someone yelled from the darkness.

"Hey, Beldon, here's a man wants tuh speak tuh you."

"One of my men callin'," Beldon explained to the girl. He raised his voice and shouted, "Who is it?"

"Baldy Brennen."

"Wait a minute." Beldon turned to Patricia. "He's the man that works nights in the hotel."

"I know," nodded Patricia.

"D'you mind if I have him come in an' talk to him here?"

Patricia shook her head.

"Not at all, Mister Beldon. I'm going to my room, so make yourself comfortable."

As soon as she had left, Beldon called, "Bring him in."

Baldy's fat fingers toyed with the brim of his hat, which he held in his lap, while he sat on the edge of a straight-backed chair. He looked nervously about him, glancing at the windows and doors with his small, pig-like eyes.

"Well, what do you want?" demanded Beldon.

"I—uh—I come here to talk business with you, Beldon."

"Get to the point then."

The fat man poked a finger in his collar and tugged at it as if it was too tight. He seemed to flounder for an opening remark.

"The—uh—that is, Beldon, the point is—I—uh—"

"If you're got somethin' to speak to me about, get to it an' be quick, or get out. I've got important things on my mind."

"Yes, I—I know it."

Baldy drew a handkerchief from his hip pocket and wiped beads of sweat from his forehead, then wiped the top of his head.

"Come over to the table where the lamp is," he said, drawing his chair close to a large, round table.

Beldon stood, resting one hand on the table's edge.

"Sit down, won't you?"

Beldon drew a chair closer and seated himself.

Baldy studied the lamp with the round glass globe that was the room's only illumination. He drew a folded paper from his pocket, opened it, and spread it out upon the table.

"Take a look at this," he said.

Beldon glanced casually at the paper, then keen interest lighted his face. He snatched the missive, read it from top to bottom, then re-read it. He looked at Baldy.

"This here," he said, "is a confession of murder. It's signed by Jake Hamill."

Baldy nodded nervously. "I know it."

"Is this genuine?"

"As genuine as a new ten-dollar gold piece."

"It's even got witnesses signed to it. This would stand up in any court. Where'd you get it?"

"I can't tell you that. You knew that Jake Hamill was one of Sam Slake's gang, didn't you?"

"Sure I know it," replied Bart Beldon vigorously. "There's a reward for his capture, ain't there?"

The Federal man drew a printed paper from his pocket and ran his forefinger down a list of names until he came to that of Jake Hamill.

"One thousand dollars reward for his capture, dead or alive," he read, "with evidence to prove his guilt."

"That's what I thought. That business about the evidence is the sticker, ain't it?"

"It has been."

Baldy gained confidence and composure.

"The law has a queer way of doin' things. It's pretty well known that Jake is a killer an' has been one of the gang of smugglers for a long time. Yet it's been impossible to prove anything against him, so he's never been captured. Now there's the proof. All you got to do is capture him. Ain't that worth something?"

Bart Beldon squinted at the fat man.

"All right," he said. "I get it now. What do you want for your part in this?"

Baldy shook his head and said, "Nothin'."

"What's behind this, Baldy? I know you ain't a public-spirited citizen. You never in your life made a move that you weren't paid for makin'. What's more, you're a yellow cuss. Now speak up."

"I'm givin' you that confession, Beldon."

Beldon looked confused.

"Well," he said. "Thanks."

He waited, wondering what was to come next, and he was not long in finding out.

"Now," said Baldy, "we come to the point of this visit. Suppose I could put a lot more of those confessions in your hands."

"Well, suppose you could?"

"What would there be in it for me?"

Bart Beldon didn't reply. He rose slowly to his feet and pushed his chair back with his heel.

Baldy looked up, saw the menacing expression in the law man's face and trembled visibly. His flabby cheeks wobbled as he began to stammer.

"Now—now, Beldon, d-don't get sore—"

Beldon's hand shot out and grabbed a fistful of the front of Baldy's coat. He jerked the fat man to his feet and held a fist beneath his nose.

"Get this straight," he said in a low, but very hard voice. "We don't make deals like you've got in mind. If you know where there are any more confessions of this sort, you're going to get 'em for me. Understand that?"

"B-but I c-can't!"

"Why can't you?"

"Th-that is, I—I got to make a deal. I don't have them now."

"What sort of deal?" snapped Bart Beldon.

Baldy Brennen was a very frightened man. He tried to explain that it would be necessary for Bart Beldon to guarantee that the government would pay the total of all rewards that were standing for the men whose confessions were turned over.

"The reward goes to the man who captures the crooks together with the evidence that convicts 'em in court of law. There ain't a word about a reward for the evidence *without* the crook! Now where'd you figure to get the rest of these confessions?"

"I—I c-can't tell. Honest I can't. I'd be killed if I told you!"

"Did you know Luther Ponsonby?"

Baldy shook his head, and his cheeks were more jelly-like than ever.

"Didn't you kill Luther Ponsonby?"

"No, no, no," cried Baldy desperately. "I never knew him. Honest I didn't."

Before Bart Beldon could hammer further questions at the hotel clerk, a clamor arose outside.

It started with a pistol shot, then a loud cry of warning. Immediately afterward there came a confused jumble of men's yells, gunshots and running feet.

Beldon gave Baldy a violent shove that sent the fat clerk staggering back across the room until he lost his balance and sprawled on the floor with a crash that made the furniture jump.

Snatching at his gun, Bart Beldon raced across the room and threw open the door. In the moonlight, less than fifty yards away, he saw a knot of struggling men.

"What's goin' on there?" he yelled at the top of his voice.

No one seemed to hear him.

He saw fists flying, then one man was lifted bodily off the ground and heaved against the heads and shoulders of the others.

The Lone Ranger was in the center of the mass of men. His voice, resonant and strong, stood out above the noise.

"Don't be a pack of fools. You men know me. I came to see Bart Beldon."

The men were too wildly excited to hear anything that was said. They fought against the flailing fists of the masked man. They yelled shrill cries of warning and sharper cries of pain. They tried to bring their guns to bear—tried to ground the stalwart masked man with a well-aimed blow by a pistol butt.

The Lone Ranger saw a gun descending, and threw up one arm to fend the blow from his head. His forearm caught the impact and sharp pains stabbed from wrist to shoulder. He lowered his head and charged to one side, bowling two men off their feet with the force of his thrust. He broke free of the ring of men that surrounded him, then whistled sharply. His voice split the night as he cried, "Here, Silver!"

Bart Beldon, meanwhile, howled at his men.

"Stand back from that man. That's the Lone Ranger. Leave him alone, you pack of crazy fools!"

But the men were hurt. Most of them had one or more bruised places where the hard fists of the masked man had landed. They were struggling to untangle themselves and recover their balance to renew the assault.

It all happened in the space of a very few seconds. The Lone Ranger got into the clear, shouted, and the white horse dashed from somewhere to his side. By the time the law men realized that he had escaped from the center of their group, he was in the saddle, guns drawn, demanding attention.

"I'll shoot if I have to," he cried. "All of you, get back and get your hands away from six-guns."

"There he is," yelled one of the men.

"I'll drop him," bawled another.

There was a shot. Flame lanced from the Lone

Ranger's gun. The law man who had started to bring his gun to bear stared stupidly at his empty hand, and saw, on the ground nearby, the weapon that had been shot aside.

"I'll take over," Beldon cried in one more effort to make himself heard.

The men looked toward the leader.

"You're a pack of crazy fools," Bart Beldon barked. "That man's the Lone Ranger an' a darned good friend o' mine. He saved my life a couple of days ago. What's the crazy idea of tryin' to kill him?"

"We didn't know who he was, boss," someone said.

"Why didn't you find out then?"

"The boys that started it didn't have a chance tuh find out," came an apologetic voice. "They just seen a man on foot comin' up to the house an' keepin' in the shadows, an' they jumped him. They figured to hammer the daylights half out o' him an' then find out who he was an' why he was comin' here. You told us that we shouldn't take no chances on Slake's men sneakin' tuh the house."

"Don't blame your men, Beldon," the Lone Ranger said, as he dismounted from Silver. "Perhaps I did look a little suspicious as I approached."

"It's a wonder to me," replied Bart Beldon, "that someone wasn't hurt."

"Yuh think someone *wasn't*," said one of the law men ruefully, rubbing a jaw that was swelling rapidly

"I mean, it's lucky someone wasn't killed."

"I didn't want to hurt any of you men," said the Lone Ranger.

"All I c'n say," went on the swollen-jawed man,

131

"is that I'm downright glad o' that. I'd hate tuh be in a fight when you was really out to do some damage!"

"Come in the house," said Beldon. "There's somethin' I want to talk to you about. A guy's in there that knows where the confessions are."

"There is, eh? Well, I've been looking for you, Beldon, because I, too, have something to talk about."

Beldon sent his men back to their posts, then led the way to the house.

When Beldon and the Lone Ranger reached the house, they found the door closed, and bolted on the inside.

"That's funny. I left the door open, when I came out," Beldon said.

A soft moan came from the house.

"That's a girl!" exclaimed the Lone Ranger.

Beldon didn't hesitate. He stepped back, then threw his weight against the door. It splintered open.

Patricia lay on the floor in the center of the room. Her lips trembled as another sobbing moan broke through them. From one side of her head, blood seeped in an increasing pool that spread out on the carpet.

An open window gave the explanation of Baldy's escape while the men outside were fighting the Lone Ranger.

Chapter XIX

THE LONE RANGER ACTS

Patricia sat in a chair near the table with a bandage around her forehead. Bart Beldon paced the floor impatiently, while the Lone Ranger made a quick repair of the damage done to the door.

The wound had proved to be only a slight, shallow cut. The skin was broken, but not deeply enough to be serious. Patricia Knowlton was angry, more with herself than with the man who had knocked her down.

"Scared to shoot him," she said in a weak, small voice. "After all my big talk."

"Now you take it easy, Miss Patricia," Bart Beldon replied. "Don't you try to talk until you're able to. I want to know just what happened here, but I c'n wait for a bit."

"I'm all right now," the girl replied.

"You're still pale, sort of."

"What did he hit me with?"

Bart Beldon held out a piece of rock the size of an egg. It was a sample of ore that had been on the table as a paper weight.

"This was on the floor beside you."

"Oh! No wonder I was knocked out."

"How'd it happen anyway? It *was* Baldy, wasn't it?"

"It certainly was, and I'll square things with him if it's the last thing I do."

"You won't need to," replied the Federal man. "I'll see that he's paid off for knockin' you down. The ornery yellow-livered rat."

Beldon turned as the Lone Ranger came from the door.

"Threw this hunk of rock at her, can you imagine an ornery snake like that?"

"You'd better get after him, Beldon," replied the masked man. "You told me that he knew where to get those confessions."

"I'm gettin' after him right away. I just want to hear from Miss Patricia about what happened."

"There's not much to tell," said Patricia. "I heard the conversation between you and Baldy. Then when you had to rush out of the house in a hurry, I came from my room. I saw Baldy locking the door and told him to put his hands up. He walked toward me as far as the table. I told him that if he didn't get his hands up, I'd shoot him. I—I guess he knew that I was bluffing. I've never shot anyone. It—it's not easy to do that sort of thing."

Bart Beldon nodded grimly.

"Well," continued the girl, "I don't remember much after that. He must have thrown that piece of ore at me and gone out the back window."

"He won't get far," promised Beldon.

He turned to the Lone Ranger.

"I'd better explain things to you in more detail," he said. It took but a few minutes to tell how Baldy had come with a proposition and how the fat man was afraid he would be killed if he told where the

134

confessions could be found. "Now I'll get to the ho-tel an' start from there," concluded Bart Beldon. "Once I get my hands on that fat polecat, I'll get all the information I want from him."

"Just a moment," said the Lone Ranger.

"Well?"

"Perhaps I can give you further information. Do you remember the man who held the knife against Patricia Knowlton's throat?"

"The critter they called Lefty?"

The Lone Ranger nodded.

"He's the one who has the confessions," he said. "I followed him from the ranch to town. He is here now, somewhere, and I'm sure he has the confessions with him."

"That settles it!" The law man started for the door.

"Hold on, Beldon, when you get those confessions, what are you going to do with them?"

"What do you think I'll do with 'em?"

"You can't arrest the Slake gang. The whole outfit has moved across the border."

"As long as I've got the evidence to jail 'em all, they'll stay there," retorted Bart Beldon.

"And Miss Knwolton will be in danger."

"Please don't consider me," put in Patricia.

"You've got to be considered. Slake isn't going to stay in Mexico any longer than he has to. You can't go on indefinitely under guard. We have already learned that Baldy was friendly with at least one member of the gang. Lefty is right here in town now."

"Well, what in thunder do you suggest?" asked Beldon sharply. "Should we give the confessions to Sam Slake when we get 'em?"

135

"You wouldn't think my plan has any merit," the Lone Ranger told Beldon. "All I can say to you is this: don't be surprised at *anything* that happens."

"What are you gettin' at?"

"Just that, Beldon. Don't be surprised, at anything."

Beldon grunted and said, "All right then."

He opened the door.

"Now I'm goin' to find a few things that the law can use."

The broken door closed behind the Federal man.

Patricia took the bandage from her head and tossed it to one side. She looked at the masked man appraisingly.

"Look here, Mister," she said slowly. "Why can't I leave here and go someplace where Slake couldn't find me? Then the law men would be relieved of the job of guarding me."

"Slake's gang is so widespread that I think you'd have a hard time getting anyplace where he couldn't find you."

"Well, what *is* to be done then? Beldon will get the evidence, I'm sure he will. Then Slake will simply stay in Mexico where he's safe, and Beldon won't be able to arrest him. If Slake gets the evidence back, he will destroy it and then all the things we've done, my father's death, everything, will be for nothing. He'll never risk keeping that evidence, if he gets his hands on it."

"That's what I thought," replied the masked man. "That's why I am afraid I'll have to do something that everyone will—" he paused and then said softly, "will hate me for doing."

Patricia looked wide-eyed at the masked man.

The Lone Ranger left the house and the vicinity without being challenged by the guards outside.

Baldy went directly to Lefty's room in the hotel and shut the door with hands that trembled with agitation.

"What's the matter with you?" snapped Lefty. "You look like you'd been chased by a ghost."

"L-lefty," began the fat man, "I—I got into an awful mess. Everything went wrong. I—I couldn't help it."

Lefty grabbed the other by one flabby arm.

"Didn't you talk to Beldon?"

"Y-yes, yes I talked to him."

"What'd he say?"

"He won't make no deal like you mentioned."

"Why not?"

"He was tryin' to make me tell where the rest of the confessions were. He was hammerin' questions at me till I didn't know whether I was on foot or horseback."

Lefty stepped back and drew a gun.

Blady's face dripped sweat. His jowls shook. He held a hand in front of him.

"Wait, wait, Lefty, don't shoot me," he cried.

"You fat rat," said Lefty. "Tell me, did you squeal?"

"No, no, no, honest I didn't."

"Did you tell Beldon where I was or who I was?"

"No!"

"What did you tell him?"

The window at the rear of the hotel was opened wide, an oversight on Lefty's part. Bart Beldon's head and one hand, holding a gun, appeared at the window. He broke into the conversation.

"Drop the gun, Lefty!"

Lefty wheeled about at the sharp command. He saw the muzzle of Bart Beldon's .44 pointed directly at his head.

"Put that shootin' iron on the table an' get your hands up. I'm here on business."

Lefty had no choice. He lowered the weapon, laying it on the table, then elevated his hands to shoulder level.

Beldon scrambled over the windowsill.

"Now," he said, "I'll take those confessions. Hand 'em over."

Lefty darted a glance at Baldy that made the fat man squirm in fear.

To Beldon, Lefty said, "I don't know what you're talkin' about."

"No? Then I'll have a look for myself. Just reach in his pockets, Baldy, an' turn each one inside out until I'm satisfied he don't have some papers on him."

Baldy looked apologetically at Lefty.

"I—I got tuh do it," he said. "You can see there ain't no choice for me."

"Rat!" snarled Lefty.

"Hurry up, I don't figure on stayin' here all night."

Baldy turned the pockets out, one after another, trembling so much that he could hardly manage the assignment. During the procedure, Lefty kept up a running string of vile epithets that were directed at the fat man, and made promises that he would square things as soon as he got the chance.

"You see," scoffed Lefty, when Baldy had finished. "I don't have anything like you're huntin'."

"I'm not through yet."

Guardedly, the Federal man reached one hand out and felt of the smuggler's shirt. A bulge, just above the belt of his trousers, brought a knowing smile. Beldon jerked at the shirt, pulled out the tucked-in part, and a leather wallet fell, with a soft thud, to the floor.

"Pick it up, Baldy."

The clerk obeyed.

"Put it on the table. It looks like the thing I'm after."

Baldy placed the wallet near Lefty's pistol.

Then it happened!

There was a shot from the window and the glass chimney of the oil lamp shattered in a thousand pieces. The light went out and three men, all of them inside the room, cried out as one.

A figure leaped into the room, charged into the trio and set all three staggering back. A split second later, the Lone Ranger was out of the room, vaulting from the window to the saddle of his horse.

"Get going," he cried. "Hi-Yo Silver! Away-y-y!"

Then a gun roared in the room.

Bart Beldon felt the heat of powder flame brushing his cheek and swung his fist without a second thought. He felt the impact as his hand met flesh and bone.

Beldon caught a quick glimpse of the masked man racing away from the hotel, in the moonlight.

It took several precious seconds to get a match lighted, locate a second lamp that was in the room, and get it lighted.

Beldon looked about him.

Baldy stood in a corner of the room, one hand

139

held to the portion of his chin that had stopped Bart Beldon's fist. His eyes were glassy.

Beldon looked at the table. The gun that had been there was in the fat man's hand. The wallet that had been there was gone. In its place there was a bullet.

Beldon picked this up.

"Silver," he cried. "The silver bullet of the Lone Ranger! *He made off with that wallet and the evidence!*"

Chapter XX

SLAKE GOES BERSERK

Lefty sprawled upon the floor, still gripping a knife in throwing position.

Baldy Brennen looked at the lean, motionless form with eyes that were wide and unbelieving. Then he glanced at the gun in his hand and his jaw slacked. He dropped the gun as if it were a thing that would turn suddenly and bite him.

Bart Beldon grasped Lefty's shoulder and turned him over on his back. In the center of his forehead there was a small hole. It took no more than a glance to know that Lefty was dead.

"Well," the law man said, "that's the end of one of the crooks."

"I didn't mean to shoot him, Beldon, honest I didn't mean it," moaned Baldy Brennen. "I never killed a man in my life. I never even shot a man. I didn't know what I was doin'. I only—"

"Shut up," snapped Bart Beldon.

"You've got to believe me though. I didn't mean—"

He broke off when he saw the way the Federal man was looking at him.

Beldon picked up the gun and stuck it in his belt. To Baldy Brennen he said, "Murder!"

"The—the man that stole the papers killed him? Is that what you mean?" asked Baldy hopefully.

"No that ain't what I mean."

"Then—"

"I mean that you're under arrest for the murder of that crook."

Bart Beldon gazed steadily at the agitated fat man. He thought a moment and then said, "Brennen, you're a skunk. There ain't a single, doggoned thing about you that's worth while. You're a yellow coward, a sneakin', sulkin', bloated worm that ain't fit to move about where self-respectin' men are. I know Lefty was a crook. He was one of the worst kind of crooks. That don't change the fact you killed a man an' if you think you can murder an' get away with it just because your victim was a crook, you're dead wrong."

"You've got to admit that he would've killed me when he got the chance, Beldon," wailed Baldy in a pleading voice. "You've got to admit that. He came here an' made me help him. I didn't want to do it, but I didn't have no choice."

"Save your breath. I'm jailin' you for Lefty's murder an' you'll get all the chance you want to have your say when you go on trial."

Brennen fell to his knees with tears streaming down the folds of flesh in his fat face. He clutched at Bart Beldon and sobbed aloud.

"Please don't jail me. I'll do anything you want. I'll help you, I'll go away, I'll do anything, only don't hold me for murder. I couldn't stand it. I don't want to be tried for murder. Nobody around here likes me, any jury that's found will hang me. I can't stand it. Please let me go."

Bart Beldon was disgusted at the exhibition of

142

abject cowardice. He felt that the man before him was something loathsome, despicable and utterly devoid of any redeeming qualities. He drew back and went to the window as if he felt the need of air from the outside.

He whistled shrilly, with two fingers against his tongue, but the signal was unnecessary because he saw two of his men coming on the run to investigate the shots they had heard.

"Take charge of that," he told the men as he pointed to Baldy Brennen who still sobbed, sitting on the floor. "Throw him in the calaboose. He's charged with the murder of Lefty."

"So Lefty's out of it now, eh?"

Beldon nodded.

"I thought I heard a horse leavin' here fast," one of Beldon's assistants said.

"You did."

"Yeah?"

"It was the Lone Ranger."

"Where'd he go? How come the shootin'?"

Beldon summarized events briefly.

"I don't know why he took the evidence away with him," he said. "Hang it all, he must have had some reason for doin' it. He always has a reason for things an' I've learned that if he's allowed to work things out in his own way, he'll come out on top. But why did he want that wallet an' the papers?"

Neither of the others could answer the question.

"You ain't goin' to let him get away with that evidence are you, boss?"

Bart Beldon looked at his assistant and said, "I don't know."

"Well, I ain't so sure that he's on your side."

"Why not?"

"He wouldn't let that Indian partner of his tell us anything when we were at the barn while it was burning. He made us leave to meet you before Tonto could say anything."

Beldon grinned slightly.

"I wouldn't worry about which side the Lone Ranger is on," he said.

"Well, I ain't worried about it, but I'm not sure that we're doin' the right thing in lettin' him get away with those papers. Why, without them, we don't have a thing on the Slake gang, an' with 'em, we can jail the whole kit an' kaboodle an' wipe out all the smugglin' in this part of the country."

Bart Beldon had a hunch and followed it up.

"Look here," he said to one of his men. "You're supposed to be pretty good on trailin' men, Jeffries."

"As good as most an' better than a lot of men," Jeffries replied. "You want me to trail the Lone Ranger?"

"D'you think you could do it?"

Jeffries looked out the window, noticed the bright moonlight, and said, "I reckon so."

"You get a horse an' start out then. The last I seen o' the masked man, he was headin' that way."

Beldon pointed with a finger.

Jeffries nodded.

"If he kept goin' I'll be able to pick up his trail outside the town. I should be able to follow it from there on."

"Get started then."

"What about him?" asked Jeffries, pointing to Baldy Brennen.

"I don't like to touch vermin like that, but Vickers and I will see that he's moved to the jail. Then

I'll go back an' make sure Miss Patricia is all right an' the men still on the job. If I'm not at my sister's house, I'll be here in the hotel. I'll be waitin' to hear what you report."

"I'll let you know as soon as I have somethin' to report," said Jeffries, as he left the room.

The Lone Ranger didn't go directly to the tree where he had left Tonto and the prisoners. He left the most direct route and turned north. In ten minutes he came to a small woods in which he knew, from previous visits, there was a cabin that had been long since abandoned.

The cabin still stood, though it was more tumble-down than ever. The door hung at a weird angle by one hinge.

He dismounted and lifted the door to one side. Cobwebs brushed his face and a musty odor filled his nostrils. There was a scurrying sound as some small animal retreated in fear of the intruder. He felt on a shelf at the left of the door and found a bit of candle.

He scratched a match and lighted the candle, then held it so wax dripped to a crude table that had been fashioned from a box. He stuck the candle upright, then sat down on another box and drew the leather wallet with the name of Luther Ponsonby upon it from beneath his shirt.

He opened the wallet and spread out the papers before him.

For a quarter of an hour, the masked man stayed in the cabin, then he blew out the candle and made a silent exit.

A short time later he rode up to Tonto's side.

"Get Slake untied," he told the Indian.

"What you get um?"

"Everything I went after."

The Lone Ranger turned to Slake.

"Slake, I'm going to show you something and I want you to tell me whether or not it is genuine."

"What is it?" asked Sam Slake curiously.

"A leather wallet filled with signed confessions."

The masked man held the wallet out while Tonto loosened the ropes.

Slake sat up, rubbing his wrists and then his ankles. He eyes were fixed upon the wallet.

"Is there light enough for you to read?"

Slake said, "No."

"Very well then, we'll build a fire."

Tonto found twigs and branches in a plentiful supply beneath the tree. It took but a few moments to get a small fire blazing brightly. Meanwhile the Lone Ranger kept a close watch on Sam Slake.

Bull complained.

"Why can't yuh get me loose o' these ropes too?"

"You stay the way you are for the time being, Bull," replied the Lone Ranger. "Slake's going to be tied again in just a few minutes." He turned to Slake. "Now get close to the fire and take a look at these confessions."

Sam Slake didn't need a second invitation. He reached eagerly for the sheaf of papers.

"Don't try dropping them in the fire, Slake," the masked man warned. "I'm watching you very closely."

"I won't."

Slake chuckled, "Here's the one you signed," he said to Bull. "Murder of the Fawcett brothers. Remember that?"

"You made us sign those cursed things, Slake."

"Good way to keep you tied to me."

Slake read the next document. Then the next.

"Are they genuine?" the Lone Ranger asked.

"Yep. Why did you think they'd be anything else but genuine?"

"I wasn't sure. I thought Lefty or Ponsonby might have been bluffing with them."

"These are the real—" Slake broke off suddenly when he saw the last few pages. He crumpled them and found his hands caught in a grip of steel.

"No you don't, Slake. I don't want those papers destroyed. Those are the most important ones of all. Those are torn from your own account books and show without question that you paid for murder, you paid for robberies and you paid for smuggling. There's one place there that tells how much you paid the men who murdered Patricia Knowlton's father."

Slake's face had undergone a transformation. All the ugliness and hate that made him the terror he was among men was vividly brought out and made more horrible by the uncertain light of the fire.

He gave a sudden jerk with strength that was surprising—strength far beyond the normal, like the strength of an insane person. He broke free of the Lone Ranger's grip on his wrists, pulling the masked man off balance. Before the Lone Ranger could recover from the surprise, Slake dove at the base of the tree, where his guns had been placed. He came up with a weapon in his hand.

Then Tonto charged. The Indian's shoulder smashed against Slake's chest with force that was like a battering ram. Slake was jolted back against the tree and his breath hissed out in a sharp gasp. He was jarred and stunned by the fury of the Indian's attack, and slumped to the ground in a daze.

The Lone Ranger took the gun from the outlaw leader's feeble grip, then took the still-held papers from the other hand.

"I guess we underestimated you, Slake," he said. "We can't take any more chances."

Slake was barely conscious.

He made no resistance when the Lone Ranger tied him for the second time. He did not fully recover until the masked man and Tonto had walked a short distance from the fire to converse in soft voices.

Chapter XXI

THE EVIDENCE DESTROYED

The moon was low on the horizon and the fire had burned down. Sam Slake feigned sleep, but he was wide awake and grateful that it had been the Lone Ranger and not Tonto who had roped him the second time. The manner in which the Indian tied a man made it not only highly uncomfortable, but practically impossible to move an arm or leg. The Lone Ranger had tied Slake's wrists and ankles but the smuggler was able to sit or lie, whichever he chose.

Bull was at his side, suffering cramped muscles, in his helpless state. Across the fire, the Lone Ranger lay on the ground, rolled up in his blanket. His regular breathing signified that he slept, secure in the knowledge that the captured men were helpless.

The masked man and Tonto had left the fire to talk in low tones for several minutes. Then Slake had seen Tonto saddle the paint horse and ride away. Shortly after that, the Lone Ranger had once more examined the papers, then stuffed them in the wallet and tucked the wallet beneath his shirt.

Slake wanted those papers. He needed the ones

that told of his own part in smuggling matters, above all else. Moreover, there was a chance that he would have the papers before long. He was waiting only long enough to make sure that Tonto wasn't nearby, and that the masked man slept soundly.

Sam Slake knew exactly how he was going to escape. His sharp eyes had spotted something on the ground, close by the fire. It was a gleaming, steely object that had probably fallen from Tonto's belt when the Indian had smashed Slake against the tree. It was a knife!

He inched his way toward it, moving without a sound, and pausing frequently to make sure of the rhythmic breathing of the masked man. It took him fully fifteen minutes to cover the ten feet of distance to the knife. But now he had the blade. He found that he could hold it with the edge toward him, then by bending his hands back, touch the sharp blade to the rope. He cut, one fibre at a time. Presently the strands gave way and his wrists were free. Then it was but a matter of seconds to release his ankles.

He lay back, motionless and tense. The steady inhalations continued from across the fire. The masked man hadn't moved. Then Slake carefully snaked along the ground to Bull and cut away the rope that held him. He held a finger to his lips in a signal of caution, then, while Bull chafed circulation back to stiffened limbs, Sam Slake recovered his weapons.

He stood, both pistols back in holsters, confident that he could control whatever situation now arose. By gestures he indicated that Bull should take his guns, then go to where the horses had been haltered on the far side of the tree.

Slake moved with the silent grace of a panther to approach the side of the Lone Ranger. He held a gun in one hand with the muzzle less than six inches from the masked man's temple. He could have fired, but this was not in keeping with his methods. Slake didn't do his killing personally. To shoot the Lone Ranger would mean that there would be a definite crime against him, and this was a thing he had taken meticulous care, throughout his long career, to avoid. He wouldn't kill, unless his safety depended upon it.

His right hand—the gun was held in the left—reached beneath the masked man's shirt and closed upon the wallet. He drew this out and felt an inward exultation as he stepped back with the most delicate part of his task completed.

He was going to take no chances of being caught before he crossed the border with those damning papers in his possession. He drew them from the leather folder, tossed them in the fire, and watched them blacken, crinkle, and finally rise as mere sparks into the air. Then he looked at Bull and grinned.

Bull returned the grin.

Now there was not a shred of evidence against any member of Sam Slake's gang. The law could be laughed at. The law could continue, as it had for years before this night, trying to get concrete evidence that would jail members of the smuggling gang.

The chest of the Lone Ranger rose and fell as he remained motionless through all of Slake's maneuvers.

Now Slake didn't care. Let the masked man waken! The evidence was gone. With Bull, he mounted, dug spurs into his horse, and headed for the Rio Grande.

"We'll get the boys," he called to Bull when they were well away from the campfire. "Now they can all go back to the ranch."

"Ain't it swell?" cheered Bull.

"I'll move 'em back to the ranch, then I'll go north an' tell Martha that she c'n come home. We'll lay low for the time bein' till the law men cool off, then we'll make plans to start operations all over again."

Bull said, "I'm so doggoned full o' bein' glad about the way things turned out, that I gotta make the welkin ring."

He snatched his gun from the holster and held it pointed toward the sky. He drew back the hammer and squeezed the trigger. Instead of the roar that would express his jubilance better than words, there came an empty click.

"Matter with my gun?" he asked. He tried again and there was another click. He "broke" the pistol, then let out a howl. "My shootin' iron ain't loaded."

Slake reined up at the edge of the water.

"Not loaded?"

"No. Take a look at your guns, boss."

Slake did so and made the surprising discovery that his weapons, in their present state, were quite useless.

He let out a bellow of harsh laughter.

"This is the limit," he cried. "Wait till the boys hear about this. If that masked man had woke up an' I had fired at him an' nothin' had come out o' my gun, he sure would o' had me! I was protectin'

152

myself with an empty gun. I should o' suspected he would o' took out the cartridges."

"Anyhow," said Bull, "it don't matter now."

"Not a doggoned bit," replied Sam Slake, as he spurred his horse into the Rio Grande to join his men in Mexico.

Chapter XXII

DISILLUSIONED TOWNSMEN

Bart Beldon rode alone. He had spent a wakeful night, trying to find an answer to the situation that had arisen. It had been a difficult problem before the masked man took the evidence, but now it was even more puzzling. The thoughts that had kept him awake persisted as he rode out of Eagle Pass, across the plains toward the Sam Slake ranch.

He had given up trying to go to sleep at daybreak. Checking with his men, he learned that the man named Jeffries had not returned. He rode, not expecting to follow any trail—he wasn't skilled at that—but with a half-formed notion that he might find some sign of Jeffries or the Lone Ranger. He had felt a need for action of some sort, so he rode. It was easier to think when in the saddle.

As long as Slake did not possess the evidence, Patricia was in peril. If Slake secured it, the law would have no cause to arrest him. Now the Lone Ranger had the papers. That is to say, Bart Beldon *thought* the Lone Ranger had them.

He tried to figure other ways that the Slake gang could be smashed.

Ahead of Bart Beldon, there was open country.

He scanned it steadily, wondering if the masked man had continued on toward the Slake ranch. He saw a solitary tree that stood apart from everything else on the plain. Then his keen eyes caught a very thin thread of smoke that rose from beneath the tree. At first he thought it was merely the haze of early morning, but as he watched it, riding nearer, he decided that it was coming from the last few embers of a campfire.

Then he saw an object on the ground, not far from the tree. It was a shapeless mass that moved. He heard his named called.

"Great Scott," he said to himself, "that sounds like Jeffries."

Beldon spurred his horse, racing toward the man who had been left, well tied, on the ground. He reached the fellow's side and leaped to the ground.

"What in the Sam Hill are you doin' here, Jeffries?"

"Get these blasted ropes off me, boss."

Beldon brought a knife from his pants pocket and slashed through the cords.

"Who roped you?"

"I don't know, but I've got plenty to tell. You been trustin' that Lone Ranger all this time."

"Why not?" demanded Beldon.

"Let me get my joints limbered up," said Jeffries, rising slowly to his feet.

He winced and groaned as he limped a few paces.

"Been here most all night," he said. "It'll take a bit to work the stiff out of my legs."

"That don't stop you from talkin'. Who roped you?"

"I said I didn't know. I followed the trail of the

Lone Ranger, like I said I was goin' to. It led to that old cabin that Lize Trombley built a long time ago. You know the place, don't you?"

"I know where it is. What'd the Lone Ranger go there for?"

"I don't know that, boss. I followed the trail, an' it wasn't so hard to follow. The moon, you remember, was bright."

"Never mind the moon. Get to the point."

Jeffries explained why he had been unable to determine what the masked man did in the cabin.

"As I came up to it, the light went out an' he rode away."

"Then what?"

"I followed him, to here."

Jeffries pointed to the tree.

"He was camped right under that tree over yonder. You can see what's left of his campfire."

"Go on."

"He had a couple of prisoners there, they were hog tied, an' one of them was Sam Slake!"

"*Slake!*" exploded Beldon. "You sure? Are you dead sure?"

"I'd stake my life on it, because of what happened."

"Well, get on with the story, what happened?"

"Well, the Lone Ranger untied Slake an' showed him the papers. They had to build up a fire so they could see them. Slake said that they were the real thing, an' then he went loco. He made a break, likely tryin' to get away, but the Lone Ranger an' a redskin that was with him, that's the one called Tonto, soon had Slake under control an' roped again."

"Yeah?"

"Well, the Lone Ranger an' Tonto walked off a little ways, then the redskin mounted his horse an' rode off. The Lone Ranger rolled up in his blankets an' went to sleep.

"Where'd Tonto go?"

"I don't know," replied Jeffries with a shake of his head.

"Go on."

"There was a knife on the ground where Slake could reach it. He cut his ropes loose, then took the wallet of papers from the Lone Ranger, drew the papers from the wallet, an' throwed 'em in the fire. He watched 'em burn!"

"What?" bellowed Bart Beldon. "You mean to tell me that all this went on under the Lone Ranger's nose an' he never woke up?"

"That's right, boss."

"Slake burned up those confessions?"

Jeffries nodded.

Beldon was almost beside himself with the things he wanted to say and the exclamations that burst from his lips. This was more than he, after the sleepless night, could stand.

"Now ravin' won't help none," Jeffries said in an effort to quiet Bart Beldon. "There's more to tell."

"There's plenty more to tell, Jeffries," burst Bart Beldon between expletives. "What were you doin' while all this was goin' on? Don't tell me you stayed right here an' watched the performance? Where did Slake go then? What about the other man that was with him?"

"I'm tryin' to tell you."

"Well, go on then, tell me."

"Slake took his partner with him. I don't know where they went, but they headed in the direction of the border. The Lone Ranger got up shortly after they'd ridden away, then he mounted his own horse an' he rode off too."

"While you sat watchin'!"

"No, I'm tryin' to cover all the things you're askin' boss, if you'll just give me time."

While Jeffries spoke, his sharp eyes were fixed on the ground as if he was looking for something.

"I was just about to go in an' throw a gun on Slake, when someone jumped me from behind. He, whoever it was, held a hand on my mouth so I couldn't make a sound. He gagged me an' roped me, an' stayed around 'till after the Lone Ranger rode away, then he cut the gag an' disappeared. I didn't get a look at him, but I got a darned good idea who it was."

"Who?"

Jeffries pointed to marks that had been made by a man wearing moccasins.

"Tonto," he said.

Beldon became silent and thoughtful.

Jeffries studied the ground for a few minutes and then suggested that he might compare the prints nearby, with those the Indian had left beneath the tree.

Beldon said, "Don't bother. I'm convinced that it was Tonto that roped you. I'm convinced of lots of things now."

"Yeah?"

"The Lone Ranger figured that the life of that girl was more important than the evidence against Sam Slake."

"But that—"

"Don't interrupt me, Jeffries. He knew that as long as we had the papers, Slake would stay south of the border where we couldn't get him anyway. So he figured that the best thing to do was to let Slake have that evidence against him. He ain't the kind to sleep when things are goin' on, any more than he's the kind to leave a knife around where Slake can get it an' cut ropes with it."

"It didn't strike me that it was like the Lone Ranger. I thought it might be someone else that was impersonatin' him."

Beldon shook his head. "It was the Lone Ranger all right enough. He knew that me, bein' a law man, couldn't return those papers to the crooks, an' he knew that if he just handed 'em to Sam Slake, Slake would be too suspicious about it. So he fixed it so the crooks would think they were puttin' one over on him, an' get the papers in the way they did."

"Gosh," grumbled Jeffries. "I guess you've got it doped out right, boss, but I hate the way things have turned out."

"That's the way it is though. It all fits in, don't you see?"

"The Lone Ranger had an idea that there'd be someone followin' him when he left the town after takin' those papers. That's why he had Tonto circle and come this way huntin' for someone like me."

"That's right," said Beldon.

He mounted his horse.

"Might as well get back to town. The boys there will be wantin' to know about things. I told 'em to stay on guard at my sister's house until they were told otherwise. Now I suppose there's no use keepin' a guard there."

Jeffries shrugged his shoulders and mounted his own horse which had been tethered nearby.

159

Back at Eagle Pass the word spread quickly. A sort of gloom descended on the town. Before noon everyone had heard about Sam Slake and the Lone Ranger.

Some agreed that the masked man had done wisely, others expressed themselves in no uncertain terms as being dead-set against letting Slake go free. Fully a dozen men grouped in front of the store and discussed the matter pro and con. In all three of the cafes there was more business than there had been in the forenoon since the last July Fourth celebration.

Everyone, no matter how he felt, whether he agreed with the Lone Ranger's act or not, had a peculiar depressed state of mind. The stories of the Lone Ranger had been recounted so many times that the masked man was looked upon as a worker of miracles. The impossible was expected of him. Even Bart Beldon had been confident that the masked rider would somehow find the way to jail the gang.

Patricia Knowlton was the most "let down" of all. She, at first, would not believe the stories.

"The Lone Ranger would never do that," she had exclaimed stoutly. "Not even if my life depended upon it. He wouldn't let killers, smugglers, thieves, and their leader, Sam Slake, go scot free! Not the Lone Ranger."

But as the forenoon advanced, the girl was compelled to accept the statements that Bart Beldon and Jeffries had made.

Bart Beldon spoke to the girl at noon.

"Don't take it too hard," he said. "The more I think it over, the more I realize that there wasn't anything else the masked man could o' done. We couldn't keep guardin' you for ever. Now we'll just have to be on the watch an' try an' get some of those crooks in the act of smugglin'. That's the only way we'll get 'em."

"You'll never get them, Beldon," replied the girl.
"I know."

"We'll try."

Patricia shook her head.

"My Dad tried for years. He had every spot on the border patrolled. He worked day and night, hopin' to get the goods on that gang. But Slake is too smart. The only mistake Sam Slake ever made in his life was in keeping those confessions. Even that wouldn't have been a mistake if Luther Ponsonby hadn't tried to double-cross him."

Bart Beldon sighed and tried to show more optimism than he felt.

"Maybe Slake won't go in for smuggling any more," suggested the girl.

"Maybe not."

"He might never smuggle another thing. He might reform. Then how could you jail him?"

"We couldn't, I guess. It'd be just about impossible to prove anything from the past."

"That's just it," said the girl with tears very close to the surface. "My father and all the others who died because of Sam Slake—they—they're somewhere, watching down on us and hoping to see their killer made to pay. Now all Slake and his gang have to do is reform and they can live for the rest of their lives on what they've taken."

Patricia Knowlton's voice grew higher in pitch as she spoke. Her face was flushed with emotion and her breath came in short spasms.

"Well, if you are going to be a bunch of mollycoddles, it's all right with me," she exclaimed. "You can't make a move against Sam Slake. You can't do anything that isn't strictly legal."

"Now, Patricia," began Beldon.

"Don't talk that way to *me!* I thought you were *men!* I thought the Lone Ranger, at least, would give Slake a fight. But no. I think everyone of you is afraid of him! Well, I'm not! I'm going to that ranch, and if Slake comes back there he's going to have to shoot it out with me. If he kills me, you can arrest him, charge him with murder! My murder! You ought to be able to prove *that!* If he doesn't get me, I'll get him. Then if you want, you can convict me of murder! You'll see what one girl will do!"

She snatched a rifle from the corner of the room and a handful of cartridges from a shelf nearby.

"I'll take Dad's rifle," she cried, "and start in where he left off!"

Beldon, silenced by the ferocity of the slender girl's outburst, galvanized into action.

"Hold on," he said, reaching for the rifle. "You ain't goin' to Slake's ranch."

"Y-you c-can't stop me," retorted the girl, breathlessly.

She fought to snatch the rifle from Bart Beldon's grasp.

"L-let me go!"

"Now you listen to me!" Beldon raised his voice to a heavy rumble. "You crazy little wildcat, if you feel that way about it, we'll go after Sam Slake."

"When?"

"As soon as we hear that he's back at his ranch. We'll put him under arrest for tryin' to hold you an' me by force an' for threatenin' our lives."

162

"And how far will any charge like that get in court?"

"It's worth tryin'."

At that moment the door swung open with a force that made both Beldon and the girl turn quickly.

Tonto stood framed in the doorway.

Patricia took one glance at the tall Indian.

"You aren't welcome here," she said angrily. "Get out."

Tonto's face remained impassive. He looked at Bart Beldon.

"You come," he said.

"Where?"

"Lone Ranger say, you go with Tonto."

Beldon paused. "I don't know," he said slowly, "as I feel like takin' any more suggestions from the Lone Ranger. You just go back an' tell him that."

Chapter XXIII

THE BIG FIGHT

Sam Slake and his men lost no time in starting back toward the ranch. The leader rode between Bull and Trigger, south of the border, following the backtrail.

Slake told and re-told the story of his escape and laughed heartily when he reached the part that dealt with the unloaded gun.

"If that masked man had woke up," he said, "I'd o' been a gone goose. But he didn't, so everything is just as it should be. I always wondered what I'd do if ever I met up with the Lone Ranger. Now I've met up with him, an' he's come out second best."

Sam Slake felt good. Two men who had caused him a lot of worry in the past few weeks were dead. He no longer had to be concerned about the betrayal that was threatened by Luther Ponsonby; neither did he have to see the gathering anger in Lefty's evil face.

He planned to discontinue smuggling for a time. In a few months, when things had quieted down and the vigilance of the Federal men had relaxed, perhaps he would start again.

There was no sign of life around the ranch. The

house was just as it had been when Slake was there the last time. The bunkhouse door was open, but nothing inside had been disturbed. Cattle grazed on a hill in the distance and everything appeared to be serene.

Slake examined the pile of charred ruins where the barn had stood. Then he returned to the house and went from room to room. He looked into cupboards and closets and then went to the basement with a lamp and examined every nook and corner.

He couldn't account for the feeling he had. The sense of well-being and assurance that he had enjoyed in Mexico had slipped away like a cloak dropped from his shoulders when he crossed the Rio Grande. In its place there was a sense of impending disaster for which he could not account.

His men noticed the care with which he inspected the place and commented on it.

"I just want tuh be sure things are as they should be," he said carelessly.

"Nothin' c'n bother us now, can it, boss?" asked Bull.

"Of course not. Didn't I tell you I burned the confessions? I watched 'em go up in sparks. That's all there was against us. The law ain't got a thing against us now."

Bull nodded and walked away.

As the day advanced the men grew increasingly restive. Usually they put in a great deal of their time in the cellar of the barn, arranging for the delivery of guns and liquor to the Indians in the north country, or sleeping. Those who slept during the day, under normal conditions, did so to prepare for a night of activity in carrying out the routine of the smuggling enterprise. Now, however, the barn was gone, and Slake had decided to remain inactive for a time. There was no use spending the day in sleep, because there would be no activity in the forthcoming night.

Some of the men tried to amuse themselves at cards. But after a short while this pastime ceased to interest them. They pitched horseshoes, grew tired of that. They polished saddles and Sunday boots, and then looked about for other diversions.

Sam Slake kept very much to himself. He tried many times, without success, to define the feeling of uneasiness. He dug some old diaries out of a tin box and pored over his past activities. While the diaries contained nothing that would in any way incriminate him, they served to recall his past. He tried to think of something that the law might have against him. There was not a thing. The more he thought about his situation, the more convinced he was that with the burning of the confessions, and his personal accounts, he had put himself entirely in the clear.

It was mid-afternoon when Slake was startled from a reverie by loud talking outside the house. He hurried to the door and looked at a group of his men surrounding a rider.

The individual in the saddle was Patricia Knowlton.

Slake hurried forward, elbowing his men aside. He stood beside the girl and squinted.

"What do you want here now?"

"I came to talk to you, Slake."

"What about?"

"It's a private matter. If you don't mind, I'd like to talk to you inside the house, where there aren't so many curious onlookers."

Bull started to laugh at the remark but the expression on Sam Slake's face choked off the humor before it began.

"What do you want to talk about?" queried Sam Slake.

"There is some unfinished business between us."

"I don't know of any."

"You will, when I call it to your attention."

The girl dismounted.

"Do we go inside, or do I have to ride back to Eagle Pass without the conference I hoped for?"

Slake stroked his chin thoughtfully without replying.

"Of course, if you're afraid I'm here to shoot you, you can have me searched and make sure I don't carry a gun into the house with me."

Slake reached his decision.

He gestured toward the door and said, "Go on."

Patricia Knowlton walked with her chin held proudly and without a backward glance. She entered the house and sat down at the table in the dining room. She remembered the room from her last visit, when Lefty had held that razor-edged blade at her throat.

She hadn't been afraid of death then. She was not afraid now. Dying held no horrors for the girl; it was only defeat that worried her.

"Will you please close the door?" she said as Slake came into the room.

The leader of the smugglers kicked the door closed with his heel. He sat in a chair, facing the girl across the table. He looked at her, waiting for her to speak.

"Slake," she began slowly, "you burned the only thing that would have sent you to jail."

Slake made no comment. None seemed to be expected.

"That happened before I could carry out the scheme I had in mind. Bart Beldon and the law men were going to try to guard me, because they thought you'd try to capture me, then hold me until you were given back that evidence. The Lone Ranger gave you the chance to get the evidence back. He did that, because he didn't want you to harm me."

Slake drew a plug of tobacco from his vest pocket and bit off a chunk. He chewed slowly and methodically, his face giving no hint of what was going on in his mind.

"Because of me," Patricia continued, "you were allowed to go free. That's ironical, isn't it?"

"Why?" asked Slake, speaking for the first time.

"Because I, more than anyone else, wanted to see you hang!"

"Why again?"

"Because you killed my father!"

"No proof of that," said Slake shortly.

"I know there is no legal proof, but you know it is the truth, and so do I. That's why I came here today. I am going to kill you!"

"You'd better think that over a little. You wouldn't get away from here alive."

Patricia laughed without humor.

"Do you think that matters?"

Her hand came up from beneath the table, holding a small pistol. She leveled this at Sam Slake.

"You won't shoot that thing, Miss. In the first place, it takes somethin' you ain't got, to shoot a man in cold blood."

"You're not a man!"

"Second place, you wouldn't have time to pull that trigger. As soon as your finger tightens on it, the gent behind you will knock you clear out of the chair."

Patricia knew, the moment she started to turn her head, that she should not take her eyes off Slake. Quickly she turned back, but Slake had already had the split-second of time he needed. His hand made a long swipe that knocked aside the pistol.

He shoved Patricia violently to one side, and made a dive for the gun. His eyes were fixed on the weapon, shining on the floor near the wall. He didn't see the tall man who stepped into the room. He wasn't aware that anyone was in the house, until he heard a resonant voice speak his name.

"Slake! Don't touch that gun."

The voice was one that Sam Slake knew. He froze, his hand outstretched. Then he turned slowly.

Patricia was the first to speak.

"The Lone Ranger!" she exclaimed.

"How'd you get here?" demanded Sam Slake.

"I was here before you were, Slake. I had quite a time keeping myself concealed while you were going through the house."

Slake recovered his composure after the first shock of surprise. He glared angrily at the masked man.

"What d'you want here?"

"Miss Knowlton told you that there was some unfinished business. That's why I'm here."

"I don't know what you're talkin' about."

"I'll tell you in a few minutes."

The masked man spoke to Patricia.

"You'd better go back to Eagle Pass."

"But wait," Patricia said. "I was there when Tonto brought your message. You are counting on—on help, aren't you? Well, there's no help coming. Bart Beldon said—"

"Wouldn't he come?" asked the Lone Ranger.

"No!"

"Does he know you're here?"

"I slipped away while Tonto was arguing with him."

"I think we can depend on Tonto."

"Now you listen to me," snapped Slake. "I want tuh know what all this talk is about. Why should Beldon come here? He ain't got anything on me!"

"That's where you're wrong, Slake," retorted the masked man. "There's enough evidence against you and your gang to hang every one of you."

"That's a lie."

"You saw the evidence with your own eyes."

"I burned it!" Slake laughed harshly. "Maybe you *didn't* intend that tuh be done. Maybe you just naturally slept through the whole thing, but that's the case, all the same. I burned that evidence in your own fire, last night."

"How do you know?"

Slake gasped in surprise. "How do I *know!* Leapin' cactus, ain't I got eyes?"

"Did you read what you burned up?"

"You showed it to me your own self. Sure I read it."

"Call your men in here. All of them."

"For what?"

"Slake, I'm finished with explaining why I want things done."

The masked man's voice took on a new, and a harder tone.

170

He came two steps closer to Sam Slake and grabbed the smuggler by one arm. He spun him around, clutched him by the rear of his collar and marched him to the window.

"Open the window," he commanded.

Slake did so.

"Now call to your men. Tell them to come in here one at a time."

"Boys," howled Slake. "Come here, one at a time."

"That's more like it."

The Lone Ranger drew Slake back, closed the window, then pushed the leader of the gang against the side wall of the large room. He drew both guns, then took up a position from which he could command the door and the wall against which Slake stood.

As the men entered, they were told to line up next to Slake.

Meanwhile, Patricia had moved to one side where she stood watching the Lone Ranger with a renewed interest. This strange man, she thought, must have some plan after all. It had been so hard for her to believe that he had shown the weakness that the evidence indicated. She wondered what would happen next. He had not seemed greatly concerned at the news that Beldon could not be counted upon to ride in with his men. Did the Lone Ranger hope to capture that whole gang, single-handed? It was hardly likely.

"Are these all the men you have here with you, Slake?"

"This is all of 'em."

"Be sure you're right, Slake. If I hear anyone

moving outside, I'll start shooting," the masked man stated flatly.

The masked man's eyes moved from one to another of the outlaws. He noticed that each man wore his guns and any one of the group would need less than a tenth part of a second to snatch a gun and fire. He tried to watch everyone at the same time.

"Should I take their guns?" asked Patricia.

"No. If you got near enough, one of them would grab you and use you as a shield."

The masked man seemed to have his plan well worked out. He gave instructions in terms that could not be misunderstood. He had the men, one at a time, draw guns from holsters, using only the thumb and one finger. The weapons were dropped to their feet on the floor. Then at the Lone Ranger's command, the smugglers kicked the guns toward him.

One of them refused, however.

"If you want it, come an' get it, mister. I ain't kickin' it to you."

"Kick it!"

"Like fun I will." It was Bull who spoke. "I know plenty about you, Mister Lone Ranger, an' one o' the things I know, is that you never shoot a man tuh kill him. I dunno why we're all takin' yore orders. You wouldn't shoot, no matter what we done."

"Very well, then. Have it your way. I don't intend to let you use that gun against me."

The gun in the Lone Ranger's right hand dropped and barked. There was a metallic *spang* of silver meeting steel. The weapon that Bull had dropped leaped across the floor, utterly ruined by the bullet the masked man had fired. Metal, little chunks of it, sprayed at Bull's feet and bit into his leg through the trousers.

The smuggler bellowed with pain.

But the instant that the Lone Ranger's attention was centered on Bull's gun gave the man at the end of the row the chance to jerk a hidden weapon from beneath his shirt.

Patricia saw him, and tried to cry a warning.

He had his gun almost brought to bear on the Lone Ranger. His finger tightened on the trigger as another roar filled the room.

The gun in the Lone Ranger's left hand jumped as it exploded. The gun that the man had tried to use jumped further. In fact, it jumped away from his hand. The man's yell of pain joined that of Bull. His hand was painfully hurt.

"Anyone else with ideas?" demanded the masked man, looking from one to another of the men. "Or will you behave as I tell you?"

"Say what you've got to say," snarled Sam Slake. "I still don't know why you're here, or what you want."

"The law men are coming to take you to jail. I didn't want gunplay. I thought, if someone was not here in the house, a few of your men would open fire when Beldon and his men ride in. That would mean that Federal men would die. It wasn't necessary to have good men die, so I came here. As to the evidence, Slake, you didn't burn it. It is true, I let you see the confessions. You took papers from the wallet while I was supposed to be sleeping, and burned those papers. I had previously taken the confessions out of the wallet, however."

Slake let out a bellow of rage. For a moment it looked as if he were going to defy the guns of the

Lone Ranger and attack. His men wore a strange assortment of expressions. Some showed anger, some surprise. Others went pale with fear.

"I was watching every move you made, Slake. If you had taken the trouble to find out whether or not your gun was loaded, my plan would probably have failed. But I didn't think you'd do that. You always boasted about the fact that you took no chances. You didn't risk opening your pistol because you were afraid the sound might waken me. You didn't risk taking the papers away with you, because you thought you might be captured with them in your possession. You see, I was quite sure you'd take no chances."

Slake's rage subsided enough to allow him to speak coherently.

"Where's the evidence now?"

"I brought it here with me. I'll hand it to the law when Beldon arrives."

Patricia Knowlton wondered if the Lone Ranger had misunderstood her when she had said that Beldon was not coming. She remembered the Federal man's manner when Tonto had brought the message and she had little hope of his arrival.

The Lone Ranger held the men in check for the moment, but how long could he keep them that way? Not indefinitely. He could not tie them. If he gave his attention to any one of the smugglers, the rest would be upon him in an instant.

The hoofbeats of a horse came from the outside.

Sam Slake cried out to his men.

"The law's comin', boys. We're goin' to hang if we're caught. We've got to fight for it."

Bull yelled, "Charge him then."

Before the Lone Ranger could speak, the men

rushed at him, closing in from all sides. He fired both guns, putting bullets in the legs of two of the men. The others fell upon him, fists swinging.

Patricia, hoping it would be Tonto arriving, raced to the door and jerked it open. Before she could cry out, the struggling knot of men smashed against the table and sent it skidding across the room.

The heavy piece of furniture hit Patricia in the side, knocking her to the floor. Her head struck the wall, as she fell, and for a moment her senses reeled.

She looked up to see the masked man in a hopeless fight. He had emptied his guns at boots and legs, wounding some of the men, but not putting them out of the fight. While they groveled on the floor, they recovered their weapons and held them, only waiting for the chance to shoot the Lone Ranger without hitting one of their own men.

The Lone Ranger swung rights and lefts with amazing speed and stunning force. Then he found himself gripped from behind, his arms pinioned to his sides. He wrenched clear of the hold and jabbed Trigger in the stomach with a fist that was still weighted by a pistol.

Bull was the one who made real trouble. Bull had leaped from a chair to the masked man's shoulders. He threw his legs about the Lone Ranger's neck, locked his ankles and squeezed with his knees.

The masked man tried to tear apart the knees that were cutting off his wind. He could not do it. He felt himself growing giddy. His breath was gone. Another instant now and he must fall.

Patricia tried to rise, she tried to reach a gun. She

was numb, unable to move. She saw the fight, the masked man's predicament, and was helpless to do anything about it.

"Oh, hurry, hurry," she breathed, thinking help might have arrived with the hoofbeats she had heard. The door swung open.

It wasn't Tonto who entered.

It was Martha Slake.

Chapter XXIV

CONCLUSION

The Lone Ranger had not been greatly concerned when Patricia said that Beldon had refused Tonto's request. The Indian could be depended upon to bring about what was desired in one way or another.

When he told Bart Beldon the Lone Ranger's ruse to trap the outlaws into returning to Texas, Beldon was inclined to be skeptical. Tonto asked the law man to step outside of the Knowlton home where they could talk without being overheard by Patricia.

It was then that, unknown to Beldon, the girl had ridden away to carry out her crazy notion to kill Sam Slake.

Tonto told Bart Beldon that there was no question about his going to the Slake Ranch. It was simply a case of the manner in which he went there.

"You go, take-um men," Tonto said. "Or you go other way, with men."

"What other way d'you mean?"

Without any trace of threatening manner, Tonto told the Federal man that he would simply rope him, and carry him to Scout, the paint horse. Then he would run off with Beldon. He would let the other Federal men see him, and they would give chase.

Beldon's face had broken into a grin at the manner in which the Indian explained things.

"You win," he said.

But it had taken Tonto longer than the Lone Ranger had calculated to persuade Beldon to go to the ranch. Even this would not have mattered greatly, if Patricia's visit had not brought things to a sudden head.

The Lone Ranger could see no hope for himself. His barely conscious mind fought valiantly against the black pit that seemed to be reaching up with taloned hands to clutch him into the depths.

He was still on his feet, partially braced in a corner. He no longer felt the pain of the innumerable blows that fell on all parts of his body.

He was only half-aware of the roar of a gun. Then the pressure on his throat relaxed and he felt the weight slide off him. He gasped, sucking in great lungfuls of air that reeked with powder smoke and dust. He saw that the men were falling back and his condition was such that he wondered why.

The gun spoke again, and he heard wild yells from Slake's men. Yells that had little meaning to him.

But his giddiness was passing now that the choking had ceased. He found his voice and cried out "Silver!"

A moment later a white fury raced through the open door. The masked man could fight no longer. His arms, battered as they were, and limp with exhaustion, could barely support the weight of his hands. But Silver came fresh to the fight.

The mighty stallion was a demon with four legs. He charged and reared, then shot sharp hoofs down in blows that would drop an ox.

Silver knew what guns were for and gave those killers no chance to use their weapons.

The Lone Ranger took a gun from the hand of Martha Slake.

He cried with new-found strength:

"Stand back and get your hands up."

Beldon came with Tonto and the Federal men when nothing remained to be done. His eyes went wide at the sight that met him in Sam Slake's house. Men were sprawled in varying positions on the floor, with Patricia doing what she could to bind their wounds. Sam Slake himself was dead. So was Bull.

The Lone Ranger didn't say that Martha Slake had been there, and gone.

The woman's story was safely locked in the masked man's heart. She had ridden back to the ranch, hoping to secure a few things she had forgotten. She had seen Slake and his men and in that moment there had risen in her a loathing and a hatred for the outlawry those men represented. Then she had ridden off.

The Lone Ranger turned the evidence over to Bart Beldon.

Beldon scanned it, then looked at the scene of wreckage and the wounded men.

"Humph," he said. "Looks to me like there wouldn't o' been a need for any trials, if we'd spent more time gettin' here."

He turned to the Lone Ranger and tried to say the many things that he felt.

The masked man smiled in a way that showed his exhaustion.

"There are too many people who contributed to the capture of these crooks," he said. "I think the one who really should be rewarded is the father of that girl."

"But Knowlton is dead."

"Nevertheless, Beldon, he's the one who first learned that Sam Slake *could* be convicted. His daughter carried on where he left off."

"But there's a heap of reward money comin'!"

The Lone Ranger said, "You'll know where that should go."

He left the house.

Bart Beldon looked at Patricia.

"Yep," he said to himself. "I know where the reward money should go—"

A voice came from outside: "Hi-Yo Silver! Away!"

Beldon listened to receding hoofbeats, then finished the sentence. "But he won't take rewards, so I reckon it will go to the girl."

America's #1 series publisher has cornered the market on the "Western" front!

EDGE
by George G. Gilman
Over 4 million copies in print!

STEELE
by George G. Gilman
Over 750,000 copies in print!

Apache
by William M. James
Over 625,000 copies in print!

THE LONE RANGER
by Fran Striker
Soon to be an international film spectacular!

THE JUSTICE SERIES
by Frederick H. Christian
"Terrific westerns . . . quite definitely among the very best stories being written by anyone anywhere!"
—George G. Gilman

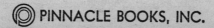 PINNACLE BOOKS, INC.